29,95

GREAT
ESCAPES

Escapes from
Natural Disasters

Stephen Currie

LUCENT
BOOKS®

THOMSON
━━✦━━™
GALE

San Diego • Detroit • New York • San Francisco • Cleveland • New Haven, Conn. • Waterville, Maine • London • Munich

© 2004 by Lucent Books. Lucent Books is an imprint of The Gale Group, Inc.,
a division of Thomson Learning, Inc.

Lucent Books® and Thomson Learning™ are trademarks used herein under license.

For more information, contact
Lucent Books
27500 Drake Rd.
Farmington Hills, MI 48331-3535
Or you can visit our Internet site at http://www.gale.com

LIBRARY OF CONGRESS CATALOGING-IN-PUBLICATION DATA

Currie, Stephen, 1960–
  Escapes from natural disasters / by Stephen Currie.
    p. cm. — (Great escapes)
Summary: Describes five natural disasters, discussing how and why each happened,
and relates the stories of individuals who survived and, in some cases, rescued others.
Includes bibliographical references and index.
  ISBN 1-59018-278-2 (hardback : alk. paper)
  1. Natural disasters—Juvenile literature. 2. Natural disasters—United States—
Juvenile literature. 3. Survival after airplane accidents, shipwrecks, etc.—Juvenile
literature. [1. Natural disasters. 2. Survival.]
I. Title. II. Series.
  GB5019.C85 2003
  940'.5—dc22
                                                                    2003012904

Printed in the United States of America

Contents

Foreword

THE NOTION OF escape strikes a chord in most of us. We are intrigued by tales of narrow deliverance from adversity and delight in the stories of those who have successfully skirted disaster. When a few seemingly chosen people are liberated from a fate that befalls many others, we feel that to some degree the larger injustice has been rectified; that in their freedom, a small bit of justice prevailed.

Persecution and disaster, whether in nature or from what has frequently been called "man's inhumanity to man," have been all too common throughout history. Fires, floods, and earthquakes have killed millions; enslavement, inquisitions, and so-called ethnic cleansing millions more. Time and again, people have faced what seems to be certain death and looked for a way out. The stories of these escapes reveal the emotional and physical strength of our fellow human beings. They are at once dramatic, compelling, and inspirational.

Some of these escapes have been entirely the work of one brave person.

Others have involved hundreds or even thousands of people. Escapees themselves vary; some seek to return to a life they have lost, others flee to a life they have only dreamed of, still others are simply fugitives against time. Their stories enlighten even the darkest events of history, making it clear that wherever there is determination, courage, and creativity, there is hope. Dr. Viktor E. Frankl, a survivor of four Nazi concentration camps, expressed this tenacity in the following way: "Everything can be taken from a man but one thing: the last of human freedoms—to choose one's attitude in any given set of circumstances—to choose one's own way."

People who are mired in captivity become willing to chance the unknown at any cost. Americans who escaped from slavery, for example, escaped toward a vision that the life they had never been allowed to live would offer them new hope. Fugitive slaves had no inkling of what life in free territory would hold for them, or if they would even make it there alive. Fears of the unknown, however, were outweighed by the mere possibility of living a free life.

While many escapes involve careful and intricate planning, no path of flight follows a fixed blueprint. Most escapes owe their success to on-the-spot improvisation and keen resourcefulness. A piece of clothing found at a critical juncture might be just the thing out of which to fashion a cunning disguise; a brick lying harmlessly in the corner of a room might provide just enough support to boost a person through the crack in a window.

Conversely, fate may carelessly toss many pitfalls at the feet of those in flight. An unexpected flood might render a road impassable; a sympathetic train conductor might be suddenly fired, replaced with an unfriendly stranger. All escapes are both hindered and helped by such blind chance. Those fleeing for their lives must be nimble enough to dodge obstacles and snatch at opportunities that might affect their chances along the way.

It is common for people who have undergone such ordeals to question whether their salvation came to them by chance, or if they were somehow chosen for a greater scheme, a larger purpose. All become changed people, bestowed with a grand sense of purpose and a rich appreciation for life. It is this appreciation for life too that draws us to their stories, as they impress upon us the importance of living every day to its fullest, and inspire us to find ways to escape from our own prisons.

Lucent's Great Escapes series describes some of the most remarkable escapes in history. Each volume chronicles five individual stories on a common topic. The narratives focus on planning, executing, and surviving the escapes. The books quote liberally from primary sources, while ample background information lends historical context. An appendix of primary sources is also included in each volume, sharing additional stories of escape not profiled in the main text. Endnotes, two bibliographies, maps of escape routes, and sidebars enhance each volume.

Introduction

Disasters and Escape

EVEN IN TODAY'S highly sophisticated and technical society, the natural world remains critical to human survival. No artificial substitutes have yet been devised for most of the basics of human life. Rivers, lakes, and underground aquifers supply the water that makes life possible. Farms and forests supply plants and animals for food. The minerals beneath the land, the air that blankets the earth, the sunlight that strikes the planet—all are vital. Without the natural world, humanity could not exist.

But nature is not always so kind. From time to time the natural world becomes extremely violent. Certain weather conditions spawn furious tornadoes with winds of 100 miles an hour or more. Sudden shifts in the subter-ranean rocks can unleash earthquakes carrying as much energy as an atomic bomb. And the combination of lightning storms and hot, dry days can create deadly wildfires, which may ravage an entire forest before finally being brought under control.

These natural disasters are always damaging to nature itself. A sudden flood can destroy miles of nearby meadows and forests; a landslide can change the contours of a mountain-side. Birds and animals are affected by changes in their habitat resulting from volcanoes, droughts, or hurri-canes, as well as by corresponding changes in their food supply. Sooner or later, nature renews itself even in the most devastated areas. Trees grow back, animals return, rivers regain their former channels. But the process is slow, and rarely are things restored just as they were.

Natural disasters can be devastating to human beings, too, especially in places where people are well settled. In dozens of ways, today's conveniences make life easier for most Americans than it was for their ancestors—and easier than it continues to be for many people around the world. But the complexity of modern life can worsen the impact of natural disasters. During a catastrophe, power lines and streetlights can become lethal weapons, and costly modern homes are much more expensive to replace when they are damaged or destroyed.

Human decisions play a role in the impact of natural disasters, too. Although no part of the earth is immune to catastrophes of some kind, people do tend to build and live in areas prone to disasters of certain types. Some of the most heavily settled areas of the United States, for instance, are also among the most likely to be struck by a hurricane or an earthquake. And there is an increasing tendency for landowners in the American West to build homes deep inside the forest, exposing themselves and their property to an increased risk of wildfire. These choices, and others like them, make people more vulnerable to natural disasters.

Rescue workers douse fires and search for victims in a building that collapsed during a 1999 earthquake in Taiwan.

Natural Disasters

For convenience, natural disasters are typically divided into categories: floods, fires, droughts, tornadoes, and so on. However, the borderline between catastrophes of different types can be very thin. Indeed, natural disasters often occur in tandem, with one triggering another. Volcanoes, for instance, can spark earthquakes; earthquakes, in turn, can set off landslides. The damage caused by hurricanes is partly due to high winds and partly due to floods that come with torrential rains. The categories are sharply defined, but the circumstances of a given disaster are rarely so neatly drawn.

The divide between natural and man-made disasters can be fuzzy as well.

Many natural disasters have been made worse by the decisions and actions of human beings. When people dam rivers and build levees, or dikes, along their banks, they do so in part to lower the likelihood of flooding. Although these attempts to control nature may work in the short term, they can create far more damaging floods a few years later. Often, decisions such as these backfire, serving only to make matters worse.

All the disasters in this book are classified as natural, since all were sparked by the forces of nature. Human activity however, played a role in making each of them more devastating—and deadly—than they might otherwise have been.

Escape

Throughout history, natural disasters have often been extremely lethal. In the course of some catastrophes, hundreds of thousands of people have been killed, and many more have been badly injured. For many who died during these disasters, death came quickly and without warning. For others, death was a long and agonizing process. As a rule, there was little or nothing any of the victims could have done to avoid their fate. The power of nature was simply too strong.

But no matter how bad conditions have become, virtually no disaster has ever killed all the people in its path. Over the years, people have managed to escape from almost every type of disaster imaginable. People have tunneled their way to freedom after being buried in avalanches. They have fought their way to safety through churning floodwaters. Again and again, they have eluded hurricane winds, found refuge from volcanic eruptions, and outrun wildfires.

Such escapes share certain characteristics. For one, they are generally unplanned. Nearly all escapes from natural disasters occur on the spur of the moment. Rarely do those who survive have the time to think out a detailed plan of action. On the contrary, if they do not respond quickly to what is happening around them, they may well die. The stories of escapes from natural disasters, then, usually involve quick thinking and no preparation.

Moreover, individual escapes from the same disaster are not necessarily alike. The circumstances of a disaster change frequently as the event unfolds, and people must seize whatever opportunity they can find to escape. It is one thing to run away from a tornado while the twister is still in the distance. It is something else entirely to attempt to flee as the tornado strikes. Each case is different; each escape is, too.

Finally, the role of luck is unusually large in escapes from natural disasters. Although many of these escapes show uncommon endurance, cleverness, and courage, the most important factor is good fortune. Those who escaped were not just skillful; they also benefited from factors beyond their control. They were the people who received a flood warning an hour or even a few minutes before the waters hit; the ones whose campsites were on the side of the volcano away from the eruption; those whose escape route was not completely blocked by rubble from an earthquake. It is undeniable that those who escaped handled their situation with courage and grace. But in every case, there was a great deal of luck involved as well.

1

Escape from the Johnstown Flood

PERHAPS THE MOST famous natural disaster in American history was an 1889 flood along the Little Conemaugh River in west central Pennsylvania. Sparked by the failure of a dam after days of heavy rain, the flood swept along the river valley and devastated the area in a few short minutes. Today the tragedy is remembered as the Johnstown Flood, named after the largest city in the path of the rushing waters. Even today, more than a century after the disaster struck, the flood is what makes Johnstown famous.

The flood was indeed tragic. Officially, the rising waters killed 2,209 people, making the Johnstown Flood among the most deadly of American natural disasters. Ninety-nine entire families were wiped out. Thousands more residents of the area were injured, many of them severely. And property damage was extensive. "One can look up the valley for miles and not see a house," wrote one reporter, surveying the wreckage after the waters receded. "Nothing stands but an old wooden mill."[1]

But despite the devastation, the Johnstown Flood did not kill everyone in its path. Some residents, alarmed when the rains grew heavy and aware of the river's history of moderate flooding, moved to higher ground before the dam broke. Others, given sufficient warning, were able to escape to safety even as the wall of water crashed down the valley toward them. And a few residents of Johnstown and surrounding areas escaped from the flood even after being caught in the worst of the deluge. Their stories rank among the most dramatic of any escapes in American history.

Johnstown and Floods

Johnstown lies in a scenic valley about fifty miles east of Pittsburgh. It is nestled at the junction of two rivers, the Little Conemaugh and Stony Creek. The city is built on a small piece of flat land wedged between the banks of the rivers and a range of mountains that rings the city. These mountains are not especially tall, but their slopes are steep, and they are set close together. As a result, the river valleys are unusually narrow.

Throughout its history, the mountains and the rivers have made Johnstown a natural flood zone. Each spring, heavy rains and melting snow combine to swell the rivers, and the steep slopes of the mountains bottle up the water. The absence of a broad floodplain, in turn, means that the excess water can spread into the streets of Johnstown and other settlements. During the nineteenth century in particular, the area experienced high water nearly every year.

The flooding certainly caused disruptions in the ordinary lives of Johnstown residents. People who lived in low-lying areas grumbled about the six inches to two feet of water that covered their streets each spring. No one much enjoyed wading to work or slogging to the store through mud and water. Families grew used to moving their furniture up to the second floor of their houses when the rains came. Still,

Changing the Land

During the nineteenth century, human intervention changed the topography of the Conemaugh Valley and made the area more prone to flooding. Not long after the region was first settled, loggers began harvesting the trees on the local mountainsides. Once, rainwater had pooled in the soil below the forests. Held in place by thick root systems and soils rich with plant life, the waters moved slowly to the rivers. By the middle of the nineteenth century, though, the root systems were increasingly disappearing—and the hillsides began to erode. Rainwater now ran much more quickly into the streams.

As people moved into the area, they built homes, schools, bridges, and factories. The more they built, the less space there was for the rivers to run over their banks without destroying valuable property. These new buildings served to narrow the river channels as they ran through Johnstown and other settlements. Like the logging, the construction had the effect of increasing the damage and scope of flooding in the Conemaugh Valley.

the floods were more an inconvenience than a disaster. The waters were rarely strong enough to destroy property or to take human lives.

Bad Weather

The winter of 1889, however, was unusually snowy. When the weather turned warm, the snow that had piled on the mountains melted. The runoff spilled into the Little Conemaugh and other area rivers, filling them above their usual spring heights. Next, spring rains deluged the countryside. Before long the soil was too saturated to soak up any more moisture. By the end of April, rainwater was flowing directly into the rivers.

Throughout the spring, between the snow and the rain, the height of the water in the Little Conemaugh and nearby waterways rose steadily. As in previous years, the flow soon overran its banks and oozed into the streets of valley communities. By the middle of May nearly a foot of water stood in the lowest-lying neighborhoods of Johnstown, and each rainy day seemed to raise the water level an inch or two. As in the past, however, area residents saw the flooding as annoying rather than catastrophic.

On May 30, though, the situation worsened considerably. That afternoon, a storm system moved into the area from the west. This system was large, slow-moving, and exceptionally intense. Late in the afternoon a heavy, driving rain began pounding the region. That evening, the clouds opened up completely, and sheets of water started to pour from the sky. This torrential rain would last all night.

Many people in the area described that rainfall as the hardest and most powerful they had ever experienced. Even senior citizens who had lived in the valley for decades could not remember so bad a storm. By one estimate, six or seven inches of rain had fallen in Johnstown alone by early morning of May 31. In some parts of the region, the figure may have been nearly twice as high. All night, the rain pounded down on the sodden valley.

By dawn, the rainfall had had a dramatic effect on the area. Water from the storm was sluicing down the mountains and pouring directly into any low-lying area available. Sometimes the water pooled into meadows and farmland. "The fields were covered with water four or five feet deep,"[2] recalled a woman who lived with her family in the mountains above Johnstown. More often, though, it tumbled into nearby rivers and streams. Early on the morning of May 31, Stony Creek and the Little Conemaugh were already running twenty feet higher than they would under normal conditions. One local newspaper editor estimated that both rivers were rising a foot and a half every hour.

Since there was no good place for the waters to go, more and more of the rivers' overflow was ending up in Johnstown. Well before dawn, the streets of the low-lying downtown district were choked with floodwaters. The

After days of heavy rain in May of 1889, the South Fork Dam collapsed, sending 20 million tons of water toward Johnstown. No one in Johnstown anticipated the danger.

front doors of some houses were entirely submerged. Schools canceled classes; factories suspended operations. By midmorning water stood ten feet high in some parts of the city. Already, this was the worst flood in Johnstown's history.

"Get to Higher Ground!"

But no one in Johnstown knew the full extent of the danger. In 1879, ten years before the May rainstorm, a group of wealthy Pittsburgh businessmen had founded a club along the South Fork, a tributary of the Little Conemaugh. To create an artificial lake for boating and fishing, club members had rebuilt an old dam along the South Fork about fourteen miles upstream from Johnstown. The dam was enormous; it was widely believed to be the biggest of its kind to be built at the time. Made mainly of dirt, it stretched nearly a thousand feet from side to side and was ninety feet thick at its base.

There were rumors throughout the valley, though, that the South Fork dam had been poorly constructed. During periods of high water, some observers pointed out, the top of the dam was only a foot or two above the

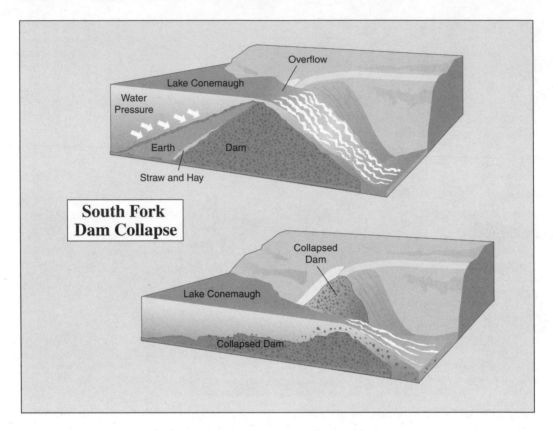

Water Pressure

Lake Conemaugh

Overflow

Earth

Dam

Straw and Hay

South Fork Dam Collapse

Collapsed Dam

Lake Conemaugh

Collapsed Dam

level of the lake. There was no easy way to release excess water to relieve pressure on the dam. And club members had cut corners in selecting their building materials. In addition to earth, the builders had used tree branches, hay, and even horse manure in constructing the dam.

Despite its flaws, the South Fork dam had withstood every rainstorm of the preceding ten years. At first the residents of Johnstown and surrounding areas had worried that the dam might collapse. But as time went on and nothing of the sort took place, they began to relax. "The townspeople," summed up one resident, "grew calloused to the possibility of danger."[3]

The rains of 1889, however, were heavier and stronger than any during the ten years of the dam's existence. The surface of the artificial lake had risen steadily throughout the spring, and when the rains started on May 30, the water was already close to the rim of the dam. By early morning on May 31, the swollen lake was rising about six inches every hour. At that rate, the waters would soon spill over the top of the dam, if the structure did not collapse from the pressure behind it first; in any case, it did not seem that the dam could last much longer.

At 11:00 A.M., John Parke, a young engineer who worked for the club, decided that the time had come to sound an alarm. Climbing onto his horse, he rode down the valley as far as South Fork, a village about two miles downstream from the dam. "The dam can't last more than a few hours!" he cried as he rode. "Get to higher ground!"[4] Some who heard Parke's warning took it seriously and headed uphill. Most, however, thought he was overreacting. Even the local telegraph operator delayed sending on the message. Because of the delay and weather-related breaks in the wires, Parke's message did not reach Johnstown for several hours.

Collapse!

As Parke had predicted, the dam did indeed hang on for a few more hours— but only a few. At 3:10 P.M., with water already sluicing over the earthen top, the dam gave way suddenly and without warning. "The whole dam seemed to push out at once," remembered a South Fork teenager who was on the scene. "Not a break, just one big push."[5] The dam, indeed, did not break so much as collapse.

Instantly, 20 million tons of water leaped forward and began hurtling down the mountain slopes. Trees on the banks snapped and were carried away by the raging torrent; boulders, loosened by the power of the water, were swept up into the current as well. A wall of water forty feet high sped down the Little Conemaugh toward Johnstown. Later studies estimated the force of the falling

John Hess's Whistle

John Parke was not the only person to give a warning of the approaching disaster. When the dam collapsed, a local railroad employee named John Hess was repairing track just upstream from East Conemaugh. When the flood struck, he and his crew were in a small locomotive, pointing toward the dam.

Hess did not actually see the flood tumbling toward him, but he heard a huge rumbling, and he saw a disturbance on the hillside ahead. As he told the story later, he knew instantly what had happened. There was no time and no space to turn the locomotive around, so Hess did the next best thing: He backed the train down toward East Conemaugh as rapidly as he could, blowing the train whistle all the way.

The people of the area were used to train whistles, but they were not accustomed to one sounding constantly. It was clear that this was a signal of danger. Given the alert, people poured out of their houses, grabbed their children, and began to head up the mountain slopes. Hess himself brought the locomotive into the train yard, tied the whistle down so it would continue to sound the alarm, and then dashed off to rescue his family. His quick thinking is credited with saving hundreds of lives.

water as equal to that of Niagara Falls.

Almost immediately, the wall of water hit a farmhouse belonging to George Fisher and his family. Within seconds the farmhouse had been reduced to splinters. Fortunately for Fisher, he had heeded the warning and made for higher ground when Parke had ridden through. Other than a few pieces of farm equipment, however, Fisher and his family saved only themselves.

Other farmers near the dam waited longer to evacuate. Some waited almost too long. George Lamb, for instance, delayed leaving his farm until the waters began pouring out of the lake. Even then, he did not immediately head for safety but decided to try to save his pigs. Only when he discovered that the pigs were out of reach did Lamb dash frantically up the hillside. He was just in time: Lamb reached safety a few seconds before the enormous wave barreled through.

Still, Lamb and his family survived. Along with the Fishers, they were the first of many who would escape the mighty waters of the flood.

To Johnstown

The flood swept down the steep and winding mountain slopes, gaining momentum and debris as it went. Below the village of South Fork, the raging waters demolished a stone railroad bridge seventy-five feet high. The town of Mineral Point, just below the bridge, was almost entirely destroyed. "I could see houses going down before it like a child's play-blocks set on edge in a row," reported one eyewitness. "[The houses would] totter for a moment, then rise, and the next moment be crushed like eggshells against each other."[6]

The flood reached Johnstown just after 4:00 P.M. Despite the telegraphed warning that had reached the city over an hour earlier, few Johnstown residents were prepared for the wall of water. As had been the case further upstream, not everyone who heard the alert believed the danger was real. Nor was there any easy way to spread the news around the city. With the streets covered with water, getting around was difficult; and most people were too busy moving their possessions to upper floors to talk to their friends and neighbors.

As a result, the flood came as a complete surprise to nearly everyone. The sight was so unusual that eyewitnesses at first mistook the waters for a dust storm, or smoke from a forest fire. "I could see a huge wall advancing with incredible rapidity," recalled one Johnstown resident. "It was not recognizable as water; it was a dark mass in which seethed houses, freight cars, trees, and animals."[7]

The waters slammed into Johnstown with astonishing force. A deluge of water thirty-five feet high and half a mile wide cascaded onto the town, covering or sweeping away almost everything it encountered. Furniture, household objects, and nearly complete

Stranded on top of wreckage, two Johnstown residents watch helplessly as raging waters destroy their community.

buildings would later be found dozens of miles downstream. So, too, would the bodies of some of the 2,209 area residents who died.

Evacuation

Despite the terrible death toll and the ferocity of the deluge, close to 95 percent of valley residents lived through the disaster. The people most likely to survive were those who lived too high up for the waters to reach. This group included most of the residents of South Fork, along with farmers in the mountains. It also included the citizens of Johnstown who lived farthest from the river's edge.

Other people in the valley survived by evacuating their homes before the dam burst. Most of these people moved in with friends or relatives who lived on higher ground. Their prudence helped them to avoid being caught in the floodwaters; yet they were the target of jokes and teasing from neighbors who had stayed behind. The people of Johnstown were proud of their ability to cope with floods, and they considered evacuation to be a sign of weakness.

Somewhat more common were people who barely escaped the deluge. Most often, these men and women saw the great wall of water barreling down on them when it was still some distance away. That gave them just enough time to run to higher ground. Like George Lamb, the farmer who had been desperate to save his pigs, many of these

people reached safety with no more than a few seconds to spare.

Six-year-old Elsie Shaffer was one of many who barely escaped being caught in the flood. When Elsie's father saw the approaching wave, he seized Elsie and her two sisters and ran. "We crossed a road and climbed a little grade," Shaffer remembered years later, "and then [the flood] struck, just that quick, as quick as you could walk across this room."[8] Shaffer, later known as Elsie Frum, lived past her hundredth birthday; but she never forgot how narrowly she had escaped the flooding.

Escape from the *Day Express*

Of the people who managed to outrace the floodwaters, perhaps the most dramatic experience belonged to passengers on a train called the *Day Express*. This train was heading east through Johnstown on the day of the flood. The high waters, though, had washed out some of the area's railroad track, and the *Day Express* had stopped at East Conemaugh, a few miles upstream from Johnstown. There it had been parked at a freight yard between the mountains and the Little Conemaugh.

For these passengers, the flooding was only an inconvenience. Like the people who lived in the valley, the passengers on the *Day Express* did not expect the waters to endanger them. They doubted that the river could get any more swollen than it already was.

Besides, they thought themselves safe in the sturdy railroad cars. As one passenger later put it, "Such a possibility as the carrying away of a train . . . was never entertained by anybody."[9]

But at 3:45 P.M. the flood came charging down the hill. A passenger named T.H. Robinson later recalled seeing the water about three hundred yards away. A few passengers, trusting in the train to protect them, decided to remain where they were. The rest, however, headed for higher ground.

The passengers' path led them across a ten-foot-wide ditch that sep-arated the train tracks from the hillside. Because of the heavy rains, this ditch was already half full of fast-moving water. A few passengers, including Robinson, came upon the ditch at the rear of the train. There they used a long wooden board as a bridge to cross the water.

But most of the passengers were not so fortunate. There were no boards where they were standing—and they had no time to make a run down the tracks to where Robinson and the rest had set up the bridge. The speed of the current made wading impossible. The

Johnstown flood survivor Elsie Frum poses with a framed print of the disaster. Frum was six when she escaped the floodwaters.

A train and an iron-works plant remain submerged beneath floodwaters. Some passengers of the Day Express *died because they waited too long to flee the stranded train.*

only recourse was to try to jump to the other side of the ditch.

Some of the passengers, mainly the younger men, cleared the gap with room to spare. One man actually made the jump with a baby in his arms. Others, in contrast, struggled. Female passengers, in particular, were weighed down by their cumbersome, ankle-length skirts. While a few women did make it across the barrier, others could not quite manage to clear the ditch. Instead, they tumbled into the current.

Fortunately, the passengers did their best to look out for one another. George Graham, who jumped the ditch early on, turned back to help those who could not quite jump far enough. "Just to my left," Graham reported later, "I saw nine women and girls tumble. I instantly grabbed the hand of the first and quickly pulled her out [while] all the others reached for me at once."[10] Although one of the women was swept from his grasp, Graham helped the other eight onto dry ground.

Even after crossing the ditch, though, the passengers were not yet safe. Refuge lay uphill, through a succession of East Conemaugh streets. Shouts and screams filled the air as terrified passengers pushed their bodies to their limits. "I ran to the second street [from the river], hoping I might be safe," recalled Robinson afterward. But the water was higher than he expected. "The houses were floating away behind me," he said, "and the flood was getting round above me."[11] Even the third street was no better: The

The Stone Bridge and Beyond

Almost the only structure in Johnstown that withstood the flooding was an exceptionally strong bridge just downstream from the city. Despite the fury of the flood, the waters could not dislodge the supports of the bridge, called simply the Stone Bridge by the locals; nor was the water high enough to surge over it.

Not only did the bridge remain standing, it also served as a barrier. Much of the debris carried down from the banks of the Little Conemaugh was swept against the bridge's seven supports. Houses, trees, and train cars all were pushed into an ever-growing pile that increasingly blocked the flow of the water.

This was not good news for Johnstown. The blockage meant that the city suffered doubly from the wave, once when the flood poured down off the mountain and again when the waters bounced back from the plugged bridge. Indeed, the ricocheting waters swept a mile or more up Stony Creek, an area that might otherwise have escaped much damage.

Many of the people caught in the flood eventually washed up on the pile at the base of the Stone Bridge. What happened to them then depended largely on luck. Some were able to pick their way across the mountain of debris and reach the safety of the shore. Others got stuck in the pile but were freed by agile rescuers who darted out onto the bridge to help. One young woman, Rose Clark, found herself trapped in a particularly gruesome way: A man beneath her in the wreckage had seized her ankle and then died, but his hand still grasped her tightly. Rescuers were able to free her.

But not all were so fortunate. There were many lit stoves in the debris that piled against the arches of the bridge, and plenty of fuel sources as well. In spite of the wet weather, a fire kindled on one of the arches and soon spread beyond it. By evening the fire was quickly consuming much of the debris. At least fifty people died in the blaze, and some sources suggest that the number was far higher.

A young woman watches as her husband and child are swept away. Johnstown residents struggled to survive as floodwaters raged through the town.

rising water still threatened to engulf him.

In the end, Robinson had just enough time to struggle past the streets and up a hillside at the edge of the town. When he next looked back, he saw that at last he was safely above the level of the flood. Half the houses of East Conemaugh were being swept downstream, along with most of the train cars from the *Day Express* and the freight yard. Although cold, exhausted, and terrified, Robinson was safe, as were most of his fellow passengers.

The Escape of Victor Heiser

The most difficult escapes, however, were made by those who had no way to outrun the flood. Many people in the Conemaugh Valley were caught up by the deluge and swept downstream. Some of these, remarkably, managed to escape death.

Among these lucky few was sixteen-year-old Victor Heiser of Johnstown, who was in a stable behind the family home when the deadly wave struck. Victor's parents, who were in the house, could not escape the deluge: The force of the water destroyed their home and killed them instantly. Victor vaulted onto the roof of the stable. Still, he felt sure the raging waters would rip the stable into bits. Believing that death was certain, Victor checked his watch; as he put it years later, "I wanted to know how long it would take me to get to the other world."[12]

But in fact, the stable was not destroyed. Instead, the whole structure was torn off its foundation and sent whirling through the waters. Given an unexpected reprieve, Victor struggled to make the most of it. He knew it would no longer be safe to keep a tight grip on the roof. To be able to breathe, Victor had to shift his own position as the stable shot forward. "Stumbling, crawling, and racing," he wrote afterward, "I somehow managed to keep on top."[13]

Within seconds, Victor saw that the waters were pushing the stable directly for a neighbor's house. At the exact moment of impact, he leapt off the stable and onto the roof of the other building—just as the walls of the neighbor's house started to collapse. As the house started to sink beneath the surface, the wreckage of yet another house came sliding by. Reacting quickly, Victor made a leap for the edge of the other house's roof. For a moment or two, he held on. Then he fell back into the waters—and landed on the roof of his family's stable, now detached from the rest of the building.

Survivors survey the damage caused by the Johnstown flood. Floodwaters uprooted homes and carried them many miles.

Clinging to his makeshift raft as it sped downstream, Victor dodged trees, iron beams, and other debris as well as he could. He could not control the roof's sideways movement, but by lifting the roof slightly he could glide over the tops of obstacles. Luck was with Victor, too. When a freight car seemed certain to crush him, a nearby brick building collapsed, changing the course of the current. "My raft shot out from beneath the freight car," Victor recalled afterward, "like a bullet from a gun."[14]

Somehow Victor managed to ride the crest of the wave to the place where the Little Conemaugh joined Stony Creek. Instead of carrying him farther downstream, the flood washed him some distance up Stony Creek. The power of the water slowed considerably once his raft had entered the creek, and before long he was able to jump to the exposed roof of a sturdy building.

Along with eighteen other refugees, Victor spent a difficult night in the attic of that building, wondering if the floodwaters would tear it to pieces. But at dawn, the building was still standing. Noticing that the waters had retreated, Victor made his way out. He crossed piles of debris and pools of dirty water to the greater safety of the hills. The flood had killed his parents, but Victor had managed to escape.

Gertrude Quinn

Like Victor Heiser, Johnstown resident Gertrude Quinn escaped from the flood after being swept up in it. Her escape was even more remarkable than Victor's, however, because Gertrude was just six years old. When the wave approached, Gertrude's father commanded his family to follow him to safety. But Gertrude's aunt, who was staying with the Quinns, was unwilling to carry her infant son through the flooded streets. Without telling Mr. Quinn what she had in mind, she stayed in the house—keeping Gertrude and the family's maid with her, along with the baby.

The two women brought the children to the attic, where they believed they would be out of reach of the floodwaters. But the wave slammed the side of the house and knocked it completely off its foundation. The floorboards and the walls broke open. Water poured inside. Gertrude watched in horror as her aunt, her cousin, and the maid were sucked down into the roiling flood. None of the three would survive the ordeal.

After crawling through a hole in the house, however, Gertrude found herself bobbing up to the surface. "I kept paddling and grabbing and spitting and spitting," she recalled afterward, "and trying to keep the sticks and dirt and this horrible water out of my mouth."[15] Her efforts were rewarded when an old mattress came sliding by. Gertrude grabbed the mattress with all her strength and climbed on.

Terrified, Gertrude screamed for help as the flood carried her downstream. She knew she was neither large enough

Johnstown sits ravaged after the devastating flood. The catastrophe killed more than two thousand people.

nor strong enough to leave her perch by herself. At first nobody came to her rescue. Possibly no one saw her; or perhaps others were too concerned with saving themselves to try to help a little girl on a fast-moving makeshift raft.

"We'll Get Out of This Somehow"

But as Gertrude barreled downstream, a factory worker named Maxwell McAchren caught sight of her. McAchren was one of about twenty people who had climbed onto a large floating roof for temporary refuge. Upon seeing Gertrude, McAchren quickly made up his mind: He could not in good conscience ignore the little girl on the mattress. Instead, despite the dangers to himself, he told his companions on the roof that he would go after the child and get her to safety.

The others on the roof tried to dissuade him, but McAchren refused to listen. Bravely, he jumped into the water and began swimming toward Gertrude on the mattress. Again and again the strong current forced him below the surface of the water. The strength of the flood also worked to push McAchren away from his goal. But McAchren was young, fit, and determined. Before long, he hoisted himself out of the water and over the edge of Gertrude's mattress. Seating himself next to Gertrude, McAchren instructed the little girl to grab his neck for safety. "We'll get out of this somehow, Miss,"[16] he told her.

The mattress, now carrying two passengers, sped downstream faster than ever. The solo swim to the raft had been treacherous enough, McAchren realized; he did not dare try to reach the shoreline with Gertrude on his back.

On the other hand, neither did he want to keep the girl on the mattress any longer than necessary. McAchren was wondering what to do when two men suddenly called to him from the window of a building just above the waterline. "Throw that baby over here," one commanded, holding his arms wide. The building was on solid ground, but it was at least ten feet away from the mattress. "Do you think you can catch her?" McAchren called back. "We can try," the man replied.[17]

McAchren unhooked Gertrude from his neck, aimed carefully, and tossed her gently to the man's waiting arms. The throw was perfect. Tavern keeper Henry Koch caught the little girl and quickly carried her up the hill to safety. The next day, she would be reunited with her father. Mr. Quinn was shocked, but overjoyed, to find that Gertrude had lived through the flood.

Gertrude Quinn, Victor Heiser, and the passengers on the *Day Express* were only a few of the people who successfully escaped from the floodwaters of the Conemaugh Valley. Had it not been for their courage, their willingness to help others, and their will to live, the death toll from the disaster at Johnstown would have been far higher.

2

The Armenian Earthquake

AMONG ALL NATURAL catastrophes, earthquakes may be the ones that happen the fastest. Whereas a forest fire may burn for a week, and a hurricane can remain highly destructive for several days, the main shock of an earthquake typically takes only a few seconds to run its course. And while the main break may be followed by so-called aftershocks—smaller, less significant waves radiating from the center of the quake—these aftershocks likewise strike in a matter of moments.

But the short duration of an earthquake does not imply any lack of violence. Indeed, earthquakes are among the most feared of all natural disasters. Large earthquakes routinely change the course of rivers, level forests, and create gaping holes in the surface of the earth where hills once stood. Moreover, they often bring about further destruction in the form of landslides, volcanoes, and great waves known as tsunamis.

The effect on humanity is equally strong. Some of the highest death tolls from any natural disaster have been associated with earthquakes. In 1976, for instance, over a quarter million people were killed when an earthquake unexpectedly struck a heavily populated section of China. A 1737 earthquake centered near Calcutta, India, is estimated to have killed 300,000, and another quake in China, this one in 1556, may have been responsible for the deaths of 850,000 people.

Earthquake Energy

Scientists express the power, or magnitude, of an earthquake by using the Richter scale, which is named after Charles Richter, the American geologist who devised it. The scale measures the amount of energy released by a tremor. Numbers range from a low of less than 1 to a theoretical maximum of 10, and are usually expressed to the tenths place; thus, an earthquake might measure 4.6, 8.0, or 7.5.

The scale is calibrated so that each integer represents ten times as much energy as the one below it. Thus, a quake that registers 8.0 on the Richter scale is 10 times as explosive as one measuring 7.0, and 100 times more powerful than one that measures 6.0.

The magnitude of the 1988 Armenian quake was measured variously at 6.9 or 7.0. Either figure represents a very serious earthquake. Generally, no more than one or two quakes a year register above 7.0, and many major earthquakes do not quite reach that level; the Northridge, California, quake of 1994, for instance, had a slightly lower magnitude of just 6.8.

Still, even the Armenian earthquake was quite a bit weaker than some other famous earthquakes throughout history. The 1976 quake in China that killed 250,000 people registered 8.0, and was 10 times more powerful than Armenia's. The earthquake that flattened San Francisco in 1906 is estimated higher still at 8.3, and the worst of a series of earthquakes striking New Madrid, Missouri, in 1811–1812 probably would have been measured at 8.7.

The strongest American earthquake to date remains the 1964 quake that struck Anchorage, Alaska. Remembered today as the Good Friday Quake, because it occurred on the Friday before Easter, this tremor was measured at 9.2—more than 100 times more powerful than the one that hit Armenia. But even the Alaska quake was not as strong as a 1960 earthquake in southern Chile. With a magnitude of 9.5, this quake ranks as the most powerful in recorded history.

Death tolls, however, are not the only way to measure the destructiveness of an earthquake. On December 7, 1988, a powerful quake hit the country of Armenia in western Asia. The Armenian quake was certainly a killer. About 55,000 people died in the disaster, the largest figure for any earthquake since 1976.

Adding to the devastation of the Armenian earthquake was the violence of the destruction of property in the region. The earthquake wiped out villages and toppled large buildings to the ground. People were trapped in schools and houses, wedged into corners, pinned beneath broken walls and crumbled ceilings. In some places, not a single building remained standing after the quake. A doctor surveying the destruction called it "a vision of horror."[18]

In spite of the carnage, thousands of Armenians managed to find their way out of the rubble. Many received help from rescue workers, friends, and family members who had not been trapped.

Many more acted on their own. Digging and clawing their way toward the light and the fresh air outside, they escaped their prison and freed themselves.

Armenia and the Disaster

The exact time and place of the December 7, 1988, earthquake could

The 1964 earthquake in Anchorage, Alaska, measured 9.2 on the Richter scale.

not have been predicted. Scientists cannot yet pinpoint precisely where and when an earthquake will strike. Still, few geologists were surprised to hear that Armenia was at the center of the disturbance. For years scientists have known that some parts of the earth's crust are more stable than others. Because Armenia lies directly atop a particularly unstable zone, it is far more likely than most other places to experience an earthquake.

Nor were the Armenians themselves unaware of the possibility of an earthquake. A 1926 earthquake centered on the city of Leninakan had caused devastation across much of Armenia, and five years after that an even more violent quake had killed twenty-five thousand in the northeastern part of the country. By 1988, most survivors of those earlier earthquakes had died. But both quakes lived on in the stories that older Armenians passed down to younger generations.

Moreover, Armenia was not the only part of western Asia subject to underground disturbances. The nearby countries of Iran and Turkey had suffered several destructive quakes since the disaster that had rocked Armenia in 1931. Shock waves from some of those quakes had affected parts of Armenia, too. And Armenia frequently experienced small tremors, too puny to do significant damage but powerful enough to serve as a reminder that the earth below the nation was far from stable.

But if residents and geologists were aware of the danger, those who governed Armenia ignored it. Although Armenia is an independent country today, in 1988 it was a part of the Soviet Union, a large and powerful federation dominated by Russia. Under the Soviet system, governmental policies were typically determined by bureaucrats in far-off Moscow rather than by local officials. When making decisions for Armenia, Soviet leaders did not seek input from the Armenians. On the contrary, government officials paid little attention to the Armenians' needs and wishes.

Armenian Architecture

Typical of the Soviet neglect was the cheap construction and bad design of new housing in urban areas of Armenia. Traditionally, Armenians had built single-story homes using stone as the major building material. They found this style comfortable and pleasing to the eye. But there was another, more practical, reason for the prevalence of this type of architecture. From experience, Armenians knew that the strong, low design could better withstand an earthquake than could taller buildings made out of weaker materials. The design was a sensible response to the reality of the place.

In the 1950s and 1960s, however, Soviet bureaucrats embarked on a massive building project inside Armenia. Against the wishes of the population, these officials rejected the idea of constructing new housing in the traditional Armenian style. Low

A man and child sit amid the debris of the 1988 Armenian earthquake. Approximately 55,000 people died in the disaster.

single-family homes, they argued, would cost too much to build and would not represent efficient use of the land. Instead, Soviet officials directed that the builders construct boxy apartment houses, most of them between five and ten stories high.

These apartment buildings might have been economical to construct, but they were not designed with earthquakes in mind. As the Armenians knew, a strong enough shock wave could topple the multistory buildings, sending bricks and beams crashing to the ground. To make matters worse, Soviet officials, eager to save money, had consistently specified the cheapest of materials and had cut corners

on safety inspections as a matter of course.

But although the Armenians knew that these buildings were dangerous, they had no recourse. A little country under the wing of the Soviet Union, Armenia was in no position to lodge an effective protest. Beginning in the 1950s, one tall apartment building after another went up. Unable to find other housing, Armenian families moved in. They could only hope that a large earthquake would not come along.

Earthquake!

Their luck, however, came to an end late in 1988. At 11:41 in the morning of December 7, a layer of rock about twelve miles below the surface suddenly shifted position. The shift released an enormous amount of pent-up energy. In an instant, the ground directly above buckled and began to shake. At the same moment, shock waves began to radiate outward from the site of the earthquake.

The break had occurred beneath a rural area about twenty-five miles northeast of Leninakan, the second largest city in Armenia and the site of the devastating earthquake of 1926. Within seconds, the first of two major shock waves had ripped through the earth beneath Leninakan—and soon after that had traveled through most of the rest of Armenia as well. The second wave, less intense than the first but still powerful enough to cause major damage, followed four minutes later.

Everywhere they traveled, the waves brought with them a terrible shaking and swaying. Hills, rivers, and man-made structures alike rocked as the earth rattled beneath them, just as had happened above the break itself. Though the waves were strongest in

Leninakan and other communities close to the center of the quake, they nevertheless could be felt throughout most of the country.

Later, a few Armenians claimed to have anticipated the tremor. Some of the warning signs they noticed were perceptible, if slight. Not far from the center of the quake, for example, some survivors said they had felt small rumblings in the earth in the days before the earthquake struck. A group of rural residents, likewise, said they had noticed a sudden rise in the temperature of the water in natural wells outside the cities. After the disaster, they attributed the change to the release of heat created miles below by the rocks beginning to pull apart.

Other signals were more difficult to define. Several Armenians noted strong feelings of unease as the moment of the earthquake approached. Leninakan resident Olga Muradyan, for example, felt unusually apprehensive on the morning of December 7. Although not ordinarily given to fearful thoughts, Muradyan decided to stay home from work that day. After the disaster struck, she wondered if she had picked up on subtle changes in the world around her that signaled the approaching earthquake.

But if these apprehensions were the result of actual signs, they were too small and vague to be preventative. Unlike some other natural catastrophes, earthquakes give very little indication that they are about to occur. There is no earthquake equivalent, for instance, of the changes in weather that mark the approach of a hurricane. Nor are quakes like forest fires, most of which occur at certain times of the year and under certain specific conditions. On the contrary, the subterranean stresses that mark the beginning of an earthquake do not generally reveal themselves until the layers of rock actually shift. That was the case in Armenia.

Shock and Destruction

Because of the lack of warning, most Armenians had no idea what was happening when the quake reached their homes. As the earth began to dip and sway, people in the affected areas felt dizzy and nauseated; but many of them attributed their feelings to stomach upsets, headaches, or other sudden illness. Even the apprehensive Olga Muradyan initially thought her discomfort was internal, rather than caused by forces deep inside the earth. "Heart attack,"[19] Muradyan remembered murmuring when she first felt the floor of her apartment building moving beneath her.

Whatever the reason for the shaking, the movement of the ground was impossible to ignore. As the shock waves snapped through the ground beneath Leninakan and other Armenian communities, buildings rocked dangerously on their foundations. Trees and streetlights tumbled; people walking in the street lost their footing and were thrown roughly to the earth. Within moments, nearly all those in the affected area realized the truth of what was happening.

Only half of a church remains standing after the Armenian earthquake. Few Armenians were warned of the approaching disaster.

This was no sudden migraine: It was a full-fledged earthquake.

In many places the arrival of the shock waves was accompanied by unexpected sounds and other disturbances. "I heard a big boom that freaked me out,"[20] reported a woman who lived in a town close to the center of the earthquake. In nearby Leninakan, residents experienced the shock waves somewhat differently: "There was a loud humming noise, then steam burst out of the ground," remembered one survivor. "It was as though the Earth was boiling."[21] Although the specifics varied from place to place,

these sights and sounds were often the first indication people had that something dangerous was happening.

But the booms and the humming noises were minor in comparison to the earthquake's effect on buildings. Within a circle extending about thirty miles from the center of the quake, the tremor toppled nearly every structure greater than two stories high—and many smaller buildings as well. In Leninakan alone, every hospital was destroyed when the shock waves pulsated through; so was every school. The nearby town of Spitak suffered even greater destruction. As a Soviet television reporter put it, the entire town was "erased from the face of the earth."[22]

In any earthquake, the potency of shock waves diminishes as they travel away from the center of the quake. As a result, the devastation from the December 7 earthquake was much greater near the center than in areas over thirty miles away. Still, the shock waves were clearly felt in the capital city of Yerevan, about sixty-five miles from the center of the quake; and more than a thousand Yerevan buildings were damaged in the tremor.

"It Wouldn't Stop"

In an earthquake, the greatest danger to human life typically comes when man-made structures collapse with people inside. For this reason, the timing of the December 7 earthquake could scarcely have been worse. At 11:41 on a December morning, the great bulk of the Armenian population

This five-story building in Spitak was completely destroyed by the Armenian quake. Nearly every building in Spitak collapsed from the disaster.

Escaping an Earthquake

As the reactions of Armenians caught in the 1988 earthquake demonstrate, many lives can be saved if people follow certain standard procedures during these frightening events. That is true on an individual level as well as on a community basis.

Doorways were the refuge of choice during the Armenian earthquake, and finding a doorway is certainly preferable to standing unprotected in the middle of a room. However, today's experts recommend seeking shelter in a doorway only when there are no other options. More commonly, people are taught to use a specific series of steps sometimes known as "drop, cover, and hold."

Upon feeling a tremor, people using this procedure are encouraged to *drop* low to the ground and hide beneath a table or other large barrier. Next, they *cover* their eyes with one hand, facing away from doors and especially windows if they can. Finally, they use their other hand to *hold* the table or object above them. The series of steps protects the eyes and as much of the body as possible from flying debris. Once the shaking has stopped, it is advisable to evacuate the building. Trying to run out the door while the shock waves can still be felt is generally considered to be unwise.

Of equal importance in surviving an earthquake is the preparedness of the community as a whole. Sound construction methods, frequent inspections, and well-defined emergency procedures can all help save lives in the event of a major tremor. As the Armenian earthquake made clear, an already bad earthquake can be made far worse by bad planning and inadequate foresight.

was indoors. The weather was too cold for homemakers and senior citizens to congregate outside. Children were in school, ten or fifteen minutes away from their usual midday recess; workers were still in their offices and factories, not quite ready to stop for lunch.

The realization the buildings were in danger of collapsing caused widespread panic among the people of Spitak, Leninakan, and other affected areas. Once the structures started to sway, there was nothing anyone could do to prevent what would follow. "It felt as if a big arm or hand just grabbed the house, picked it up and started to shake it harder, and harder, and harder," reported survivor Sevak Minasyan. "It wouldn't stop at all."[23]

The swaying of the buildings disoriented people and made movement difficult. There was every likelihood that walls and ceilings would shake apart—or that an entire building would sway off its foundation altogether. Those people who lived in the tall apartment houses of Leninakan and other cities worried that they would suddenly be tumbled eight or nine stories to the ground.

But if the people of Armenia could not control the shaking, they could control their response to it. Through earthquake drills in schools and at home, for example, Armenians had been taught to take refuge beneath a doorway as soon as the earth began to rumble; the top of a door's frame can help shield victims from falling debris. Remembering these instructions, many Armenians immediately took refuge in the nearest doorway. While not all those who found a doorway survived the disaster, it is certain that many lives were saved by this maneuver.

Those who could not reach a doorway found some other kind of shelter. "Our [only] protection was a table," remembered Sevak Minasyan; Minasyan and his wife were visiting a neighbor couple at the time of the tremor. "When the earthquake hit, all four of us ducked underneath the table. It wasn't much protection from all the things that were landing on top of it but it was standing and that's all we were hoping for."[24] The Minasyans and their neighbors were fortunate. The table protected them from most of the debris, and all four of them survived the quake.

Escaping to the Outside

Clearly, staying under a table or in a doorway was not a long-term solution. As buildings rocked and swayed, it quickly became apparent that safety lay only in escaping from these doomed structures altogether. For some, escape was relatively straightforward. That was especially true for those who lived in the low, sturdy houses traditionally favored by Armenians. Residents of these buildings could run directly out the front door, either as the house continued to rock or—if the house survived the initial shock—once the shaking had subsided. Ideally, they would be safe in a matter of seconds.

For those who lived in the upper floors of apartment houses, in contrast, escape could be extremely difficult. The ground floor was several flights of stairs below their apartments. Nor was reaching the ground floor any guarantee of finding an exit. Even if a building did not collapse, doorways and lobbies could quickly fill up with concrete blocks, electric wires, and other barriers.

Maro Gharibyan was one who wasted no time in finding a way out. When the earthquake hit, Gharibyan was standing at the balcony window of her fifth-story Leninakan apartment; her mother-in-law and four-year-old son were also home at the time. The earthquake's first shock wave knocked Gharibyan down, but she managed to grab her son and crawl along the tilting floor to an interior doorway. The older woman could not reach the doorway and so remained in the middle of the room. Fortunately, the wave did not tumble construction materials down on top of her.

As soon as the earth stopped shaking, Gharibyan made a dash for the apartment's front door. She pulled frantically on the door's handle, but bricks

Rescue workers carry the body of an earthquake victim in Leninakan. Some Armenians did not have time to leave their buildings before they collapsed.

and pieces of ceiling had crashed to the floor on both sides of the doorway, preventing the door from swinging on its hinges. For a few seconds Gharibyan panicked. It seemed impossible to get the door open.

"Half of the Stairs Were Gone"

But Gharibyan did not give up. Instead, she enlisted the help of her mother-in-law. Together, the two women tugged on the handle and tried to yank the heavy door toward them. When that failed, they attacked the door with their

hands and feet, kicking and pounding it as hard as they could. The door suddenly flew open, and the three hurried out to the landing.

The path down the stairs was barely navigable. In many buildings, including Gharibyan's, the stairwells had partly filled with fallen rubble. As in the apartments themselves, potentially deadly objects from loose ceiling tiles to concrete blocks were raining down from above. On the stairways, too, some of the steps had been dislodged in the earthquake. "Half of the stairs were gone,"[25] recalled Gharibyan years afterwards about her experience. As she, her son, and her mother-in-law started down the steps, they knew it would be essential to watch their footing.

Clutching her son and running alongside her mother-in-law, Gharibyan bolted down what was left of the stairway. Like others in similar situations, the group avoided placing their feet in the places where the steps had vanished and clambered over piles of concrete blocks. They descended past the lower floors one by one, all the while half expecting to feel the rest of the building tumbling down around their heads. But it did not. Together, they burst into the front lobby and through the unblocked front door. Then they stepped out into the cold winter day.

Outside, buildings lay in ruins. Survivors wept in sorrow and stood gaping at the wreckage. The sounds of screams and sirens filled the air. But for

Little is left of a three-story building in Leninakan. As buildings collapsed, the people inside them realized the only escape was to get outside.

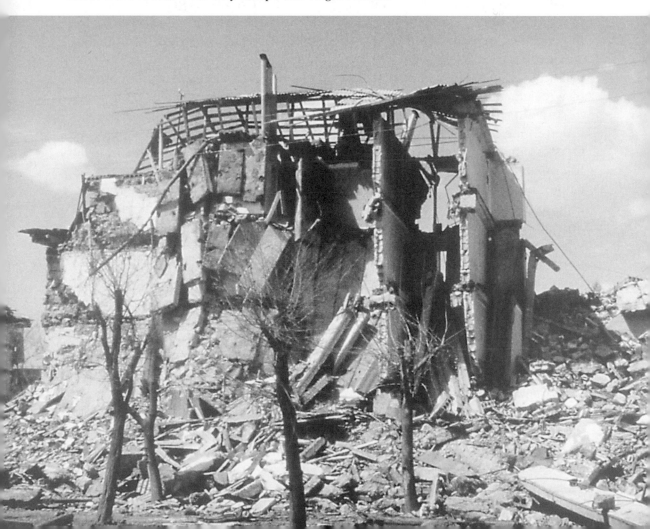

the moment, at least, Gharibyan and her group were safe.

John Oganesyan Escapes

Not all buildings stayed intact long enough for people to escape. Some structures collapsed almost as soon as the shock waves arrived. In other cases, the extent of the damage made immediate escape impossible. College professor John Oganesyan, for instance, was in his third-floor office when the earthquake struck. The tremor quickly leveled the entire structure, collapsing the upper floors of the building onto those below. In an instant, Oganesyan and the two friends who were with him had tumbled to the basement, with tons of wreckage all around them.

Amazingly, none of the three was killed in the fall, nor even badly hurt. Oganesyan cut his knee when a block fell on his leg, and his foot was briefly caught between two heavy rocks. But though they were alive and relatively uninjured, the men were uncertain whether they could make their way out of the rubble.

At first, in fact, the three men decided to stay where they were. The basement was pitch dark. Moreover, concrete blocks and other debris towered above their heads, much of it balanced only precariously. If they tried to make their way to the surface, the men reasoned, they risked being crushed in a shower of concrete. Besides, they thought, help might be on the way.

For the next few hours, the men remained wedged into a tight triangle several yards below ground level. But as time passed and no one came to their assistance, Oganesyan and his friends decided that climbing to the top was their only option for survival. They hoped it would be physically possible to find a path that would lead to the outside. They knew they would need to move carefully enough to avoid toppling the unstable debris all around them.

Slowly and laboriously, Oganesyan and his friends began their climb. Cautiously they crawled over metal beams and slid upward through the small spaces between concrete blocks. They hoisted themselves onto broken pieces of furniture, and they pushed and pulled one another around piles of shattered brick. Despite the appalling circumstances, the men were fortunate in one respect: One of Oganesyan's friends had a few matches in his pocket. Striking them one at a time produced enough light for the men to see, roughly, where they were going and what obstacles lay ahead.

One step at a time, the men moved upward. Before long they could see daylight through the debris in front of them. Encouraged by the sight, they hoisted themselves up onto the level of what had been the building's first floor and made their way to the pile of bricks that had marked the outer wall. People were visible on the sidewalk beyond this rubble, and the three friends shouted to them. Within minutes,

Former tenants collect belongings in what used to be their homes. Thousands of Armenians were left homeless after the quake.

bystanders had knocked a hole in the bricks large enough for the men to squirm through.

Courage and Luck

In a sense, there was nothing especially unusual about the escapes of John Oganesyan and Maro Gharibyan. Dramatic as they were, both escapes were common in the first hours of the Armenian earthquake. Hundreds of thousands of people fled their homes in and around Leninakan when the earthquake struck. Despite circumstances as difficult and dangerous as those faced by Gharibyan and Oganesyan, most of them survived.

Thousands of Armenians, for instance, had frantic flights of their

Pulled from the Rubble

Not all those who survived the Armenian earthquake escaped under their own power. Many of the survivors were too badly hurt to extricate themselves from the rubble that surrounded them. Some were knocked unconscious; others, though mostly uninjured, were too small, weak, or fearful to find a way out; and still others were pinned beneath the wreckage and unable to move. "I tried somehow to free myself," recalled one man, as quoted in Yuri Rost's *Armenian Tragedy*, "but I only had partial use of my right arm."

Those trapped under the debris had one chance for survival: rescue workers. Soon after the disaster, teams of rescue workers began combing the affected area, listening for cries and other signs of life. Some of these rescue workers were highly trained professionals, many of them flown in from other countries. Other groups were hastily organized from among local residents who had escaped the worst effects of the quake.

The effectiveness of these groups varied considerably. Even at the time, observers criticized the government for a lack of preparedness. There was a shortage of power equipment, so many of the rescue teams, especially those provided by local authorities and the Soviet Union, had to rely on crowbars, hammers, and their bare hands to move debris. Nor was there time to train everyone in proper procedures. In a few cases, the efforts of well-meaning but uninformed rescuers actually cost lives.

Still, no one questioned the commitment of the rescuers. In the days after the earthquake, according to some estimates, up to fifteen thousand people were extricated from the ruins of the fallen buildings. The last were pulled to safety more than a week after the tremor took place. The rescue operations added significantly to the overall survival rate.

Survivors stand in the rubble of their destroyed neighborhood. For most survivors of the quake, it was blind luck that allowed them to escape with their lives.

own down apartment building stairways just before the multistory dwellings collapsed. Across Leninakan from Gharibyan's apartment, a homemaker led her elderly mother and two small children to safety from the ninth floor of her building. They reached the outside moments before the entire structure fell in upon itself. Olga Muradyan, the woman who had felt oddly uneasy on the morning of December 7, made it successfully downstairs and outside her building while the walls tumbled down around her. Their stories would be repeated again and again throughout the affected area.

Many of the survivors took the time to rescue or alert others. One man was in the basement of his apartment house when the earthquake struck. His wife and small children were stuck on the fourth floor, however, so he dashed up the steps to help his family escape from the building. Similarly, one of Olga Muradyan's neighbors took the time on his way downstairs to kick on doors elsewhere in the building. "Run for it!"[26] Muradyan recalled him calling to their fellow residents.

Escaping from the rubble was somewhat less common than running out of buildings, but many people saved themselves by doing what John Oganesyan had done. Finding a way to safety, however, was not an option for everyone stuck under the debris. Some were trapped in the wreckage, unable to move due to injury or the position of the rubble around them; these people had to be freed by rescuers, or else they would die. Still, hundreds of Armenians caught in the ruins of their homes, offices, and schools managed to pick their way through the debris to safety.

Courage played a large role in these escapes. It took great courage for Maro Gharibyan to risk running down the damaged staircase; it took courage for John Oganesyan and his friends to leave the rubble in which they were trapped. Those too frightened to take these chances were less likely to survive. In many buildings, those on the upper floors decided to stay where they were. The result, for most, was catastrophic. When the buildings collapsed, as many did within a few minutes of the earthquake, the people were killed instantly.

Luck also played an important role in determining who escaped and who did not. Olga Muradyan had time to get out of her building because of circumstances she had done nothing to bring about. Unlike several nearby apartment houses, her building survived the initial shock wave, affording her and her neighbors the chance to escape. The same was true of Maro Gharibyan. Both were lucky, as well, that the stairwells of their buildings had not been totally destroyed before they ran outside; elsewhere in Leninakan, debris made stairs impassible even as the buildings remained standing.

John Oganesyan was even more fortunate. Many others who fell a similar distance were killed upon landing, or were crushed by concrete blocks that fell on top of them. Even those who survived a similar fall found themselves badly injured, wedged in by debris, or otherwise unable to move. Indeed, most survivors attributed their escapes more to good fortune than to their own efforts. As much as any natural disaster, the Armenian earthquake demonstrates the importance of both luck and courage in making successful escapes.

3

The Fire at Storm King

OF ALL NATURAL disasters, fire is perhaps the most unpredictable. Weather conditions, ground cover, and a host of other factors can turn a slow-moving, seemingly harmless fire into a whirling blaze in an instant. Sudden and unexpected gusts of wind can change the direction in which a fire moves; a new source of fuel can make a small fire burn hotter and at a faster pace. Those who fight wildfires—a term that refers to any fire that burns across mountains, forests, or other types of natural terrain—must constantly be on guard as they work.

In the early days of fighting wildfires, deaths and serious injuries were quite common. Today, they have become much more rare, mostly because firefighters have developed new equipment, new strategies, and better understanding of the way fires burn in the wild. Fires are still extremely dangerous, however, and firefighting efforts are directed toward saving lives. As a commander put it recently while preparing to lead a group of firefighters into a mountain blaze, "Nothing we're doing today is more important than a human life."[27]

Nevertheless, the nature of fires means that tragedy can still strike at any time. "Firefighting is not chess," observes a journalist; "it is not a logical endeavor in which good strategy always prevails."[28] No matter how carefully firefighters observe safety procedures, or how accurately authorities predict the path of a fire, there is no guarantee that a wildfire will behave predictably. When a wildfire does the unexpected, the men and women who are fighting it must escape its fury as well as they can. Among the most dramatic of these escapes took place in July 1994 on Storm King Mountain in Colorado.

The Wildfire Begins

On July 2, 1994, a lightning bolt struck a tree somewhere on Storm King Mountain. The lightning sparked a small fire that spread gradually through the woods and brush on the mountain's slope. At first, however, no one was terribly con-

cerned about the blaze. Wildfires like this are common in the Colorado mountains, and the fire on Storm King was small, moved slowly, and did not immediately threaten any people or buildings. For the first few days after the fire ignited, in fact, officials in charge of firefighting in the area more or less ignored it. The spring and early summer had been hot and dry, and there were bigger, more dangerous fires to worry about.

The decision, however, had consequences. As one nearby resident pointed out afterward, the initial blaze could have been extinguished by one

The Storm King fire began when a lightning bolt struck a tree on the mountain.

firefighter with a shovel and a small tank of water. Neglected, however, the fire grew in strength and size. Three days after it ignited, the blaze covered much of the southwestern slope of Storm King. By now it was too big to ignore, especially because this slope adjoined an interstate highway and was close to two towns. On July 5, officials began to send firefighters to the area to limit and extinguish the blaze.

That was not an easy task. Storm King is difficult to access. The mountain itself is steep, rocky, and covered with trees and brush. The few trails in the area were inappropriate for vehicular traffic, so it was impossible to bring in fire trucks and other heavy-duty firefighting equipment. Officials would have to use other methods to attack the fire on Storm King Mountain. Fortunately, authorities were prepared to be flexible.

Smokejumpers and Hotshots

In the western United States, fires often spring up in inaccessible stretches of wilderness far from roads and supply centers. Because these wildfires cannot be fought by means of standard firefighting equipment, experts have developed specific ways of battling these blazes. One common method, for instance, is to drop either water or fire-retarding chemicals on the fire from aircraft passing over or hovering above the site.

Storm King or South Canyon?

The devastating Colorado wildfire of 1994 is usually known as the Storm King fire. The name makes sense; after all, Storm King Mountain was the site of the blaze. However, a few sources refer to it as the South Canyon fire instead.

"South Canyon" was the name originally given to it by firefighting officials. An early report on the blaze erroneously placed it several miles away from Storm King Mountain, and the mistake was not formally corrected until much later. By then, the fire had become newsworthy, and some reporters and other observers had grown accustomed to calling it the South Canyon fire. Even today, "South Canyon" is sometimes used to identify the fire.

Still, water is not usually enough to extinguish a raging wildfire, and aircraft crews cannot always drop their loads with precision, especially when the weather is windy and the terrain is steep. It is usually necessary to call in a specialized group of firefighters trained to deal with wilderness conditions. If it is feasible, some of these firefighters hike to the fire site from roads and trails in the area. On Storm King, for instance, the first seven firefighters on the scene walked up a gully on the southeastern side of the mountain, crossed a ridge, and were at the fire after a hike of less than three miles.

In some cases, however, it is quicker and more effective to transport firefighters to the affected area by helicopter. If the terrain permits, the helicopter can land to discharge its passengers; if not, the firefighters parachute into the wilderness. These firefighters are collectively known as smokejumpers. Most smokejumpers work in small groups, with their partners changing from one fire to the next. A few, however, are organized into tight units of about twenty firefighters each. These units train together and fight fires as a group. Members of these units are usually known as hotshots. Both smokejumpers and hotshots travel wherever their services are most needed.

The seven firefighters who had hiked in on the morning of July 5 were soon supplemented by several other crews. Later that afternoon, eight smokejumpers from Montana and Idaho parachuted into the area. On the following day, another group jumped in to join them. Finally, the force was rounded out by the arrival of the Prineville Hotshots, an elite firefighting squad based in Oregon. The Prineville team came in by helicopter, landing at one of the two makeshift helipads hacked out of the wilderness by the smokejumpers. By the early

A smokejumper leaps from a plane to fight a wildfire. Smokejumpers and hotshots came from three states to control the Storm King fire.

afternoon, there were forty-nine fire-fighters on the slopes of Storm King Mountain.

The men and women at the scene of the blaze that day did not attempt to fight the fire directly, as their urban counterparts do. Instead, their assignment was to control it as best they could by cutting it off from its fuel sources. To this end, the firefighters tried to create a fire line, or a clear space, surrounding the burning area. The fire could burn up to the edges of the fire line without interference, but the blaze would eventually consume all the brush, grass, and wood inside the fire line. Then, unless a strong wind or another unexpected event carried a stray ember across the line, the blaze would burn itself out.

To create the fire line, the crews on Storm King Mountain carried equipment such as chain saws, shovels, and pulaskis—a tool that combines features of axes and hoes. Each person also carried food and water, along with a small aluminum tent known as a fire shelter to serve as protection of last resort. If a fire threatened to overwhelm a group of smokejumpers, they could deploy their tents and crawl inside the metallic shielding designed to offer protection from the heat.

"An Ugly Little Creeper"

But in the early afternoon on July 6, none of the forty-nine men and women on Storm King expected to have to use a fire shelter. The fire seemed ordinary enough: Brad Haugh, one firefighter at the scene, described it as "just an ugly little creeper."[29] The strategy was simple enough, too. One group of firefighters stayed on Hell's Gate Ridge, which the seven original firefighters had hiked across; this ridge marked the top of the burning slope. Their job was to cut brush and trees to form a fire line. Ideally, this line would keep the fire below Hell's Gate Ridge and on just one side of the mountain.

The other firefighters were assigned to cut a second fire line down the slope. This line would start at the cleared area on the western end of the ridge and continue along the western flank of the fire. When these crew members arrived at the lowest point of the fire, they changed direction and headed across the steep slope of Storm King to hook the line around the base of the fire. They expected to be able to continue hacking their way back up Hell's Gate Ridge on the opposite edge. The maneuver would create a fire line of at least eighteen inches, sometimes more, around the hundred acres or so that were then ablaze.

Moreover, the firefighters on Storm King Mountain had taken plenty of safety precautions. Every crew member carried a portable radio to alert others to problems. There were emergency meeting places, such as the helipads at the top of Hell's Gate Ridge and the gully on the ridge's other slope. Besides, the firefighters knew they had to be constantly aware of their surroundings. All

Firefighters monitor a controlled burn. Firefighters deliberately set smaller fires around a wildfire to remove sources of fuel.

had been trained to keep "one foot in the black,"[30] as firefighters say, meaning they are ready to duck to safety into the burned area that can no longer support a fire.

But while no one thought that this fire would create particular problems, not a single firefighter at the scene was taking the blaze lightly. One veteran hotshot describes fighting wildfires as "dodging dead trees . . . rocks falling on you, breathing thick smoke, not knowing where you are"[31]—and that description holds even under the best of circumstances. Although the crew

members were without exception in excellent physical condition, the stress took its toll.

The crew members were also aware that conditions could change in a matter of a few seconds. The greatest danger in fighting wildfires is the possibility of a giant blowup, a dramatic explosion of the flames caused mainly by abrupt changes in the wind. In theory at least, a blowup could occur at any moment. Still, it seemed unlikely. Large-scale blowups are not especially common. Besides, even moving uphill and loaded down with gear, most firefighters can outrun all but the most quickly moving wildfires. There seemed to be no reason for alarm.

Firestorm

By 3:30 on the afternoon of July 6, the forty-nine firefighters were scattered across the southwestern slopes of Storm King. Nine, all of them smoke-jumpers, were at a rocky outcropping which they called Lunch Spot Ridge. This ridge was on the eastern side of the fire and about seven hundred yards below Hell's Gate Ridge at the top of the mountain. Another twenty-two crew members were stationed on top of the ridge, where they cleared the area and occasionally ferried supplies down to the men and women working below.

The other eighteen crew members were widening and clearing sections of the fire line that had already been constructed. Five were working along the upper reaches of the fire line, though still two or three hundred yards below the ridge. This group included Brad Haugh, a Colorado firefighter employed by a government agency called the Bureau of Land Management, and Kevin Erickson, a smokejumper from Montana.

The final group was near the bottom of the line. Like those on Lunch Spot Ridge, they were about seven hundred yards below Hell's Gate Ridge, but they were along the west flank of the moun-tain rather than the eastern slope. Although most of these crew members belonged to the Prineville Hotshots, four

were smokejumpers. Among the most experienced of these smokejumpers was Eric Hipke, an exceptionally athletic firefighter from the state of Washington. A tall and muscular man who bicycled and played ice hockey in his spare time, Hipke was one of the most physically fit firefighters on the mountain that day.

Shortly before 4:00 that afternoon, a cold front moved across the area. It brought with it high winds, which stirred the flames of the fire sprawling across the southwestern slope of Storm King. Stoked by the wind, the flames leaped higher and burned more strongly. Gradually at first, and then with increasing speed, the fire began to spread.

Initially, none of the scattered fire-fighters knew exactly what was going on. "We knew we were having some trouble,"[32] recalled Brad Haugh. But like most of those on the mountain, Haugh believed that they were dealing with an isolated flare in their section of the mountain. No one had a view of the entire fire. Indeed, at first many of the firefighters made no particular prepa-rations to escape. They simply started walking away from the strengthening blaze.

Within a minute or two, though, the fire had swept completely out of con-trol. The flames cascaded to the bottom of the slope and set fire to a stand of extremely flammable oaks. Spreading to the side and gathering strength, these flames then headed back up the moun-tain toward the fire line being created below the western end of Hell's Gate

A colossal firestorm engulfs a road and wooded area. The Storm King crew had to run up the mountain to escape the fire.

Ridge. At the same time, the main body of the fire grew in intensity and started rolling up the hill to Hell's Gate Ridge itself. In both cases, the wall of flame was pushed by winds estimated at fifty miles an hour and assisted by the heat, the dry conditions, and the steep slope of the mountainside. The blowup had begun.

"It Sounded Like a Tornado"

At about 4:00 in the afternoon the seriousness of the situation became clear to almost everyone on the mountain. Radio communications between the scattered groups made it evident that the flares were much more widespread than anyone had guessed. For most of the firefighters on the mountain, the signs of a full-scale blowup were now unmistakable. "[The fire] just exploded," remembered Brad Haugh. "It sounded like a tornado."[33]

From his post on Hell's Gate Ridge, Prineville superintendent Tom Shepard could see the fury of the firestorm more clearly than most. Shepard was deeply concerned about the safety of those along the western flank of the fire line. These crew members had been instructed to head farther down the mountain if the fire should become dangerous. But the fire's rush to the bottom of the slope had cut off this potential escape route.

The firefighters' only chance, Shepard knew, was to run up the moun-

tain. Unfortunately, the southwestern side of Storm King Mountain slopes to the top of Hell's Gate Ridge at angles approaching forty-five degrees, making the climb an ordeal even for the most physically fit. The trees and the tangled underbrush simply added to the difficulties. And the inferno stirred up by the winds was moving much more quickly than wildfires typically travel.

Shepard was not sure that the crew members along the fire line recognized the danger. Grabbing a radio, he made contact with the firefighters below him. "Get out of there," he instructed the group. "Abandon the fire line."[34] He told the group to make their way up the mountain as quickly as they could. Then he signed off. There was nothing more he could do to help them.

The firefighters on the line obeyed the superintendent's orders and began the climb up the mountain. Despite Shepard's warning, however, they did not fully understand the urgency of the situation at first. The fire did not advance quickly in their area. Lulled by the slow movement of the flames, and tired after a long day of fighting the blaze, the group did not hurry to safety as quickly as they should have. Firefighter Eric Hipke later recalled that he initially felt little fear of the smoke and flames.

But as he walked on, Hipke began to worry. Messages began coming over the radio from other firefighters stationed all over the mountain warning that the entire slope seemed to be on fire. As they moved up the mountain,

The Peshtigo Forest Fire

The worst forest fire disaster in American history took place in 1871 at Peshtigo, Wisconsin. Over a thousand people were killed; many more were injured in the tragedy. In some ways, perhaps most notably in the size of the death toll, the Peshtigo blaze was quite different from the Storm King fire of 1994. In other ways, however, the two fires were very much alike. Certainly, the fires were similar in that some people who seemed sure to die in each blaze nevertheless made dramatic escapes from the flames.

The disaster in Peshtigo began in hot, dry conditions similar to the fire at Storm King. On October 8, 1871, the fire whipped through much of the densely forested region and spread to the little town of Peshtigo, smoke billowing through the sky. Terrified and given very little warning of the upcoming disaster, the people of Peshtigo knew they could not outrun the fire. Instead, they hurried to the local river, also called the Peshtigo. Their idea was to jump in, cool their bodies, and stay beyond the reach of the flames.

As it happened, the river was not a place of complete safety. Although the flames could not jump across the water, the searing heat of the fire radiated across much of the channel. Hoping to avoid the heat, the people of Peshtigo ducked under the water, with the idea of surfacing only when they absolutely had to breathe. Some found this impossible; of these, many were burned to death when the flames scalded their faces and lungs. But others managed to remain in the river, taking small, quick breaths when they needed to, until the fire had burned to black and they could once more go onto the shore.

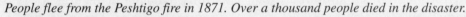

People flee from the Peshtigo fire in 1871. Over a thousand people died in the disaster.

Hipke and the other members of his group noticed an increase in the size and intensity of the smoke and flames. The blaze was neither as isolated nor as small as it had appeared to be.

Up the Mountain

Among those worried about the group on the fire line were Brad Haugh and Kevin Erickson. Haugh and Erickson had been stationed along the fire line themselves, but a good deal farther up. With the fire still some distance away, they stopped near a large pine tree to wait for those coming up the slope from below. They knew the climb was steep and exhausting, and "[the crew members] were walking at a slow pace," Haugh recalled after the fire, "tools still in hand and packs in place."[35] They thought they might be able to assist the crew members as they neared the ridge. "Let's give [them] a little support," Haugh told Erickson, "grab a saw or lend a hand."[36]

Unfortunately, the group below Haugh and Erickson was moving slowly. The angle of the slope and the tangled underbrush both worked against the firefighters. So was the sheer number of crew members in the group. The fire line was scarcely wide enough for even one person to traverse it comfortably.

Thus, those at the rear of the line were forced to move at the pace of the slowest person ahead. Moreover, dips, curves, and ridges on the trail slowed down trailing members of the group twice: once when the head of the line encountered an obstruction, and once when they reached it themselves. The result was a constant series of bottlenecks.

About three or four hundred yards below Hell's Gate Ridge, Hipke's group happened upon a spur ridge—an unusually steep section of the trail. As they picked their way up the slope, the fire behind them gained speed. Later researchers estimated that the flames converged on the crew at a rate of about five miles an hour—nearly five times faster than the group could travel at this point. Hipke had not fully recognized the danger until this moment. Now, he realized the seriousness of their situation.

So did Haugh and Erickson, standing near the pine tree on higher ground. A minute or so earlier they had caught a glimpse of the winding column of firefighters ascending the mountain. Directly behind the oncoming firefighters, though, they saw a wave of flame shooting up the slope. Haugh and Erickson frantically urged those below to hurry, but by this time they needed no encouragement. "I saw them beginning to run," Erickson recalled, "with fire everywhere behind them."[37]

Several firefighters in the line decided to stop and deploy their fire shelters. But Hipke, like a few others, continued to run. He did not believe that the shelters would keep the crew members from harm. The terrain was largely unburned, and shelters are designed to withstand heat rather than flames. Instead, Hipke decided to take his chances with the climb up the mountainside.

Erickson and Haugh turned to run. They had almost left it too late themselves. Later, Haugh would estimate that the fire spread from the tree up to the top of the ridge in twelve seconds or less. They scurried forward, their legs and lungs stretched to their fullest capabilities; and even that was almost not enough. "So this is what it's like to run for your life,"[38] Haugh remembered thinking as he hurried up the mountainside.

Scrambling up the steep slope just behind Haugh and Erickson, Hipke

Escape from Lunch Spot Ridge

The smokejumpers on Lunch Spot Ridge knew they were in an awkward situation when the blowup occurred. They believed they had little chance of reaching Hell's Gate Ridge from their location below. The steep and rocky route up the slope led through large stands of unburned territory—trees, brush, and grasses that were likely to catch fire. While there was a zone of already burned "black" some distance up the hill, the smokejumpers feared it might prove too small to be a refuge against the approaching inferno.

But there were no real alternatives. Below them and to one side, the fire raged; the other side was a long stretch of unburned forest that seemed likely to be ignited and, in any case, did not lead to safety. The group on Lunch Spot Ridge quickly agreed to try the slope. "I moved out as fast as my stubby little legs could carry me," recalled firefighter Quentin Rhoads, as quoted in John Maclean's *Fire on the Mountain*.

Together, the firefighters scrambled up the steep slope of Storm King, grabbing for rocks and branches in an effort to stay ahead of the fire that was chasing them. Dropping their equipment as they ran, they covered several hundred yards before the fire caught up to them. That was enough. Although the group was still at least a hundred yards below Hell's Gate Ridge, the firefighters had reached the black area they had been aiming for. Better yet, it was significantly larger than they had expected.

Given the size of the blackened zone, members of the group decided that their best chance of escape lay in riding out the blaze in their fire shelters. Quickly, they deployed their tents and crawled inside. It was a wise decision. The metallic outsides of the shelters deflected the heat and kept those inside from burning as the fire roared up the mountainside. Once the blaze had passed, the firefighters who had been on Lunch Spot Ridge crawled out of their tents. They were shaken, but they had survived.

A fire crew retreats from the flames of a wildfire. Even the most experienced and physically fit firefighters are at risk when fighting wildfires.

felt the searing heat of the fire on his back. Just short of Hell's Gate Ridge, a blast of hot gases from the fire washed over his body, choking him and severely burning his hands and neck. Still, he continued. Throwing himself forward over the top of the ridge, he rolled to his feet and ran down the other side of the slope to the spot where Haugh and Erickson were waiting.

Each of the three had sustained injuries in the blaze; each was exhausted and terrified. But for the moment, at least, all three were safe.

Hell's Gate Ridge

When the fire erupted, the men and women on Hell's Gate Ridge were in a better position than the firefighters on the slopes below. One reason was that those already at the top of the mountain were farther from the flames than Hipke and the rest of those on the fire line. Moreover, they did not need to expend valuable energy running up the slope toward safety.

Still, Hell's Gate Ridge was by no means a place of refuge. There was no burned-over zone to prevent flames from reaching the crew members near the top of the ridge. Nor was the cleared fire line wide enough to set up shelters. And the suddenness of the blowup, along with the speed of the fire, negated the advantage these firefighters had by being atop Hell's Gate. "I remember looking out from the ridge and just seeing clear [sky]," said hotshot Louie Navarro. "As I looked back five seconds later, the whole skyline was completely black."[39]

Although the flames did not arrive immediately, heavy smoke quickly surrounded the firefighters on Hell's Gate Ridge, stinging their throats. Butch Blanco, the commander in charge, quickly told crew members to head for

the safety of one of the two helipads. These zones, which had been cleared of vegetation, had already been designated as possible places of refuge. And a few of the firefighters, including Blanco himself, did manage to reach H2, the more northern of the two landing spots.

But most of the firefighters on the ridge headed instead for the other helipad, H1. As they converged on the cleared area that marked the landing spot, a sudden burst of flame attacked the trees standing beside the safe zone. Later, hotshot Bryan Scholz would describe the flames as "a nasty orange,

A raging fire consumes trees and a home surrounded by flames. The H1 helipad offered no refuge to firefighters fleeing Hell's Gate Ridge.

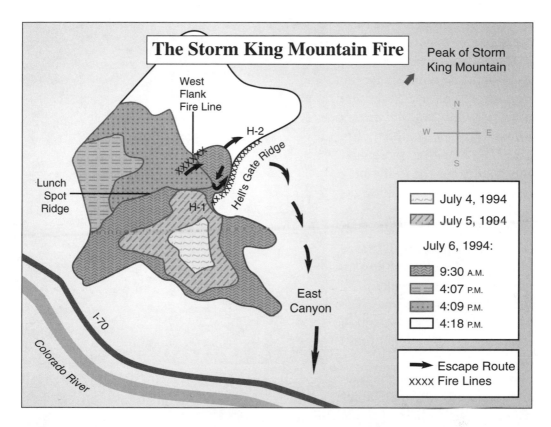

The Storm King Mountain Fire

Peak of Storm King Mountain

West Flank Fire Line

H-2

Hell's Gate Ridge

Lunch Spot Ridge

H-1

East Canyon

I-70

Colorado River

N
W — E
S

July 4, 1994
July 5, 1994

July 6, 1994:
9:30 A.M.
4:07 P.M.
4:09 P.M.
4:18 P.M.

→ Escape Route
xxxx Fire Lines

a malignant orange . . . just a deadly orange base with a black wall [of smoke] on top of it."[40] There might have been safety at H1, had the firefighters arrived there, but the flames now made it impossible to reach the helipad.

"Snowing Ash"

Not only had these firefighters lost precious time in trying to make it to H1, but the attempt had put them in an extremely dangerous position. Their only hope now lay in running back along Hell's Gate Ridge in the direction from which they had come. Flames pursued them from behind and below much speed, and no matter how the group was able to summon, it seemed that the flames moved more quickly still. "I'd never seen anything like it, that big, that close,"[41] remembered another hotshot, Brian Lee.

In theory, the firefighters could have escaped the fire by heading down the opposite, eastern side of the ridge, where Erickson, Haugh, and Hipke were standing; the flames had not yet reached that part of the mountain. But along this part of the ridge, the drop into the gully was unacceptably steep. The group plunged ahead at a breakneck pace toward the junction of the ridge with the fire line on the western flank of the mountain. At this spot, known as a saddle, the drop into the eastern canyon was gentler.

Desperate to outrun the blaze, the group sprinted along the ridge, stumbling over rocks and stumps. A few fell, but others stopped to help them up. Breathing became more and more labored as the firefighters wearied and the smoke thickened. "It was snowing ash,"[42] remembered firefighter Kim Valentine. Worse, small blazes called spot fires had sprung up here and there, sparked by embers blown by the wind. The path to safety led past—and in some cases through—these small fires.

Still, the only hope was to hurry forward. As the flames careened down the ridge, the firefighters managed to stay a step ahead of the inferno—but only barely. Louie Navarro later recalled watching two crew members running through an "arch of fire."[43] Later, those on the ridge estimated that the flames might have reached a height of 150 feet. Despite the speed and size of the fire, however, every crew member who had tried to reach H1 made it safely to the saddle.

Into the Canyon

Once at the saddle, the firefighters turned right and dropped down into the canyon on the eastern side of Storm King. This was the area where

Crosses on Storm King Mountain memorialize the firefighters and helicopter pilots who perished in the Storm King fire.

Erickson, Haugh, and Hipke had taken refuge, along with those who had initially reached H2. For the moment, at least, the flames remained on the edge of Hell's Gate Ridge. That gave crew members a chance to hurry down the slope and put distance between them and the blaze.

Their escape, however, was not yet complete. Spot fires had already begun on the eastern slope, and there was every chance that the main blaze would pour over the ridge and down the other side. If it did, the firefighters would be no better off than before. And even though they were largely heading downhill, the rocky terrain did not favor quick movement. "It was hard ground to move in," remembered hotshot Bryan Scholz. "We did a lot of falling."[44]

Moreover, by now the firefighters were exhausted. Many had acquired bruises or worse injuries on the way into the canyon; nearly all had suffered from smoke inhalation. Hipke's hands were badly damaged. Several others stumbled along slowly, pausing to rest from time to time. Banged up as they were, it was all they could manage.

Yet the knowledge that the flames were close behind them spurred the firefighters on. In the face of the danger, no one was left behind. Other firefighters bandaged Hipke's hands as best they could. Louie Navarro grabbed one man by the back of his neck and hustled him along. Bryan Scholz pulled Kim Valentine down the slope.

It was well that they hurried. Within an hour after the group had begun to make its way out the eastern canyon, the Storm King fire did indeed spread to the eastern slope of the mountain. Flames rushed down the unburned slope of Hell's Gate Ridge as quickly and ferociously as they had rushed up the other side. But by then, the firefighters who had headed down the mountain had nearly reached the highway.

One by one, the firefighters filed out of the entrance to the canyon, where they were met by emergency personnel. They had successfully escaped from one of the most ferocious wildfires of their era.

Tragedy and Relief

The escape from the Storm King fire, however, was tempered with sadness. Of the thirteen firefighters at the front of the fire line that day, only Hipke survived. The other twelve died not far from Hell's Gate Ridge—one just a few feet from the summit. Some were caught by the flames as they struggled up the slope. Others died in their shelters, or in the act of deploying them. Two helicopter pilots were killed, raising the death toll to fourteen, when they chose to try to reach the summit of the mountain rather than going down into the eastern gully.

Today, the Storm King blaze is best known for the loss of so many brave firefighters. No wildfire in the recent history of firefighting has been more tragic. The tragedy, however, is not the entire story. The escapes are important, too. Had it not been for the courage, cool heads, and physical stamina of the other firefighters on the mountain, far more people could have been killed. Given the intensity and suddenness of the blowup, and the speed with which the flames advanced, perhaps the wonder is not that so many died—but that so many more escaped.

4

Escape from the Frank Landslide

FOR MOST NORTH Americans today, landslides are among the least familiar of all natural disasters. Few people can name more than one or two famous landslides throughout history; most cannot name even one. While earthquakes, volcanoes, and floods are well known and frequently reported, landslides seldom make the news.

There are several reasons for this. For one, truly large landslides, at least in North America, are rare. For another, since the sliding of rocks down a mountain typically affects only the slopes and the area immediately below, even enormous landslides are limited in their effects. And for a third, landslides tend to occur so deep in the backcountry that it is rare for people to be injured.

But despite their low profile, landslides—or "slides" as they are sometimes called—can indeed be dramatic. Those who have witnessed tons of rock shearing off a mountainside describe it as among the most remarkable sights imaginable. Landslides are abrupt, usually occurring without any apparent warning. And they are quick; most are over within a minute or two. The suddenness and speed of landslides can leave witnesses wondering if what they saw actually happened.

The devastation caused by a landslide, too, can be remarkable. During a slide, fields and meadows are covered in thick piles of rock, rubble, and debris from the mountain slopes. Rivers fill; forests are buried. More than almost any other kind of natural disaster, slides make permanent changes to the land. Flowers and trees will reclaim land flooded by a nearby river, and forests will regenerate themselves after a wildfire has swept through. But the boulders from rock slides will alter the original landscape for centuries—perhaps forever.

Because landslides can be so destructive, and because they can occur so unexpectedly, it is extremely difficult to escape from the fury of these disasters. The crashing rocks can obliterate everything in their path, and the speed with which a slide travels makes it almost impossible to outrun. As a result, the stories of people who escape from landslides rank among the most remarkable of all escapes from natural disasters. Of these, one of the most dramatic took place in 1903 in the Canadian Rockies.

Coal and Turtle Mountain

In 1903 the community of Frank was a small but lively town on the Canadian frontier, nestled in the Rocky Mountains in what is now the province of Alberta. Founded in 1901, by 1903 the town already had a population of about six hundred. And most observers believed that it would continue to grow in size and importance.

The business of Frank was coal, at the time the single most valuable source of fuel in North America. Coal was plentiful in the mountains surrounding the village; in fact, coal was the reason for Frank's founding. In 1901, a cor-

poration called the Canadian-American Coal and Coke Company had opened a mine inside Turtle Mountain, just south of where the village would be built. Frank sprang up to serve as a home for the men the company hired to work the mine. Other businesses quickly moved into town, hoping to capitalize on the wealth the coal might provide. By 1903, Frank was home to a bank, a weekly newspaper, several hotels, and other small businesses unrelated to the mine.

There was every reason to expect continued prosperity. The Turtle Mountain mine was certainly productive. One of its owners called it "the world's richest coal mine,"[45] and though this was an exaggeration designed to bring in investors, it was not off by much. Turtle Mountain was home to a very thick seam, or deposit, of coal. Deep inside the mountain was a twenty-foot-wide swath of what one observer described as "solid, glistening, jet black coal."[46] By early 1903, the miners had dug a main tunnel over a mile into the middle of the mountain, and they were pulling out thousands of tons of coal every day.

They were assisted in this work by a quirk of geology. The coal seam at Turtle Mountain ran more or less straight up the center of the mountain. Once inside the mountain, the miners simply broke the coal above their heads, and stepped aside to let gravity take over. Trolleys were positioned down in the main tunnel to receive the pieces. Most other mines required

Coal miners stand at the entrance to a mine in the early 1900s. The town of Frank was comprised largely of miners who worked in Turtle Mountain.

workers to dig deep into the earth and haul their coal up to the level of the tunnel, but the miners in Turtle Mountain did not have to carry out this laborious step. Spared the heavy lifting, the miners could process more coal in less time than otherwise would have been possible.

Not that mining Turtle Mountain was easy. The miners worked long shifts in cramped, poorly lit quarters where the air was often stale and dusty. They loosened tons of coal with pickaxes, crowbars, and other hand tools, helped by occasional blasts of dynamite. They lived in fear of cave-ins, explosions,

and unexpected releases of deadly gas deep within the mountain. Even in Turtle Mountain, mining was dangerous, demanding work, and it was carried out under the most uncomfortable of circumstances.

Still, mining was the best job option open to many North American men at the time, and there was no shortage of men looking for work in the Turtle Mountain mine. By 1903 about two hundred men were working regularly in the mines during the day. A skeleton crew of about twenty monitored the mine at night, checking the wooden supports that kept the ceiling from caving in, handling any necessary repairs, and generally ensuring that the day crew would be able to start work as soon as it arrived.

The Abnormal Geology of Frank

To the miners and the mine owners, the coal deposit was what made Turtle Mountain most interesting and important. To be sure, local residents also appreciated the mountain for its beauty and majesty. Its craggy face overlooked the town of Frank, and its peak rose sharply to an altitude about three thousand feet above the community. Viewed

from the town, or from the Crowsnest River that ran along the valley, the height and breadth of the mountain were truly impressive.

To a geologist, however, the mountain would have been interesting for reasons that went beyond its beauty and its coal. Turtle Mountain was oddly constructed. It was formed millions of years ago, and its upper and lower halves were quite distinct. The mountain's summit was made of limestone, one of the harder rocks to be found in the area. Its base, in contrast, was made up of softer rocks, notably shale and sandstone in addition to the coal.

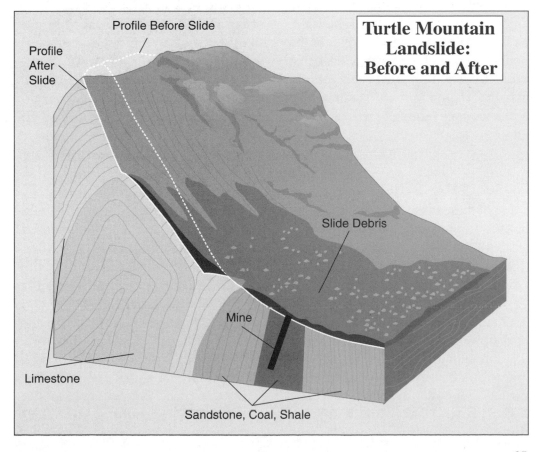

Profile Before Slide

Profile After Slide

Turtle Mountain Landslide: Before and After

Slide Debris

Mine

Limestone

Sandstone, Coal, Shale

For most of the mountain's existence, the difference had not mattered much. But in modern times, the mountain had become top-heavy. The soft rocks at the base of the mountain were easily eroded by wind, rain, and the workings of the river. But erosion worked much more slowly on the harder limestone on the mountain's top. Little by little, the base of the mountain wore away, while the summit remained much as it was.

By 1903, the top of the mountain was noticeably larger than what lay below. Once, the mountain would have presented a smooth, seamless face from the summit to the ground. But as the bottom of the slope slowly disappeared, the limestone face on the top half of the mountain gradually became a ledge that stuck out over the rocks beneath. Early visitors to Turtle Mountain commented on the way the mountain seemed to jut out at the top.

Was Frank Safe?

A few of these visitors, moreover, noted that the Indians who lived in the area kept their distance from Turtle Mountain. According to the Native Americans, small pieces of rock were forever falling off the summit of the mountain and tumbling down its slopes. Someday, they feared, the entire top of the mountain might shear off and slide down into the valley. Indeed, the Indians generally referred to Turtle Mountain as "The Mountain That Moves."[47]

The Indians were not alone in their concerns. Even several scientists who studied the mountain agreed that instability was present. Coal company engineer Raoul Green, who saw Turtle Mountain for the first time soon after the mine opened, recalled that the mountain seemed to be "hanging loose—just ready to come down."[48] Territorial mines inspector William Pearce also harbored doubts about the stability of Turtle Mountain.

But at the time, no one raised any kind of an alarm. No one tried to shut down the mine; no one encouraged the new residents of Frank to move farther from the mountain's shadows. For no one really believed that a devastating landslide could occur. Later on, even Green would say that he had anticipated only a small-scale slide, perhaps one in which a few tons of rock slipped off the summit and came to a stop along the mountainside.

Economic concerns certainly played a role in the silence of Green and others. No one in Frank wanted to disturb the community's sudden financial success by questioning the mine's safety. Yet even allowing for the clouded judgment of those who depended on the mine for their livelihood, it seems evident that few people in Frank seriously considered the possibility of a major disaster. For most of the town's new citizens, the question of safety simply was not an issue.

An earthquake caused this 2001 landslide in El Salvador that destroyed every home in its path. The damaged caused by the Turtle Mountain landslide was even more severe.

The Mountain Tumbles

The mountain, in fact, was even less likely to hold than Green and Pearce believed. Millions of years of erosion had increasingly destabilized the top of the peak. The mining, too, may have worsened the problem by weakening the mountain's interior. Weather conditions played a role as well. In the spring of 1903 a series of warm and rainy days was followed by subzero temperatures on the night of April 28–29. As a later report on the disaster put it, "The fissures in the mountain [probably] filled with water, on which

the frost would act with powerful effect."[49] The frozen water pushed outward, increased the size of the splits in the rocks, and weakened the structure of the mountain.

Whatever the exact cause of the slide, however, Turtle Mountain began to come down at 4:10 A.M. on April 29. In that instant, an enormous wedge of limestone suddenly and unexpectedly detached itself from the north face of the mountain and began to slide toward Frank. As the limestone barreled down the slope, it picked up speed and mass. The power of the tumbling rock scoured the mountainside, scraping up trees, stones, and soil and dragging them along. Within a few seconds, a massive landslide was pouring down the side of Turtle Mountain.

The rock did not stop somewhere along the slope, as Raoul Green had hoped. The slide had too much power for that, and too much weight as well. An estimated 90 million tons of rock came crashing toward the valley at the base of Turtle Mountain. As one historian writes, "The rock ploughed through the bed of the Crowsnest River, carrying both water and underlying sediments along with it, crossed the valley and hurled itself up [another mountain] to a height of four hundred feet."[50]

The sound of the slide could be heard dozens of miles away, though at first few had any idea what it was. One nearby resident thought it was an explosion, another a rifle shot. "Somebody must be having a real party,"[51] one man remembered joking to a friend as they traveled home after a dance; at the time, they were one hundred miles north of Frank. Others reported hearing strange whistling sounds as the rocks poured down the mountain, like the escape of steam under pressure; and many noticed a shaking in the earth or a violent gust of wind.

Although the slide lasted only about a minute and a half, the valley and the mountain had changed dramatically.

Casting Blame

At heart, the Frank Slide was due entirely to natural causes. The erosion of the bottom of the mountain had created an unstable situation, and as one report pointed out, the sudden freeze on the night of the landslide had widened the cracks in the rocks, thus destabilizing the mountain. At the time, most people in and around Frank were content to leave it at that: The disaster had been no one's fault.

Some people, however, cast blame on the mining operations as well. "Of the various causes which were responsible for the big slide," one geologist wrote flatly, as quoted by J. William Kerr in *Frank Slide,* "there can be no question but that the mining of coal was a prime one." He and others argued that the mining had weakened the mountain and created extra stress, thus hastening the collapse. Indeed, the part of the mountain that fell was directly above the coal seam.

Today, geologists generally agree that the weather played a small role in the disaster, and that the mountain's structure played a very large one. There is much more debate about the impact of the mining on the landslide. The actual degree to which the mining was responsible may never be known for sure.

The north slope of Turtle Mountain was swept completely bare. At its feet lay a pile of rocks and rubble, covering most of the valley to an average depth of forty feet. In some places, stone was piled one hundred feet above the valley floor. Over half a mile of the river was completely filled in; any suggestion of a channel lay buried beneath tons of massive rock. The Frank Slide was the largest landslide in modern Canadian history.

Escape Below

As a group, the people of Frank were fortunate that night. The landslide missed the central section of the town, where most of the population lived. To be sure, the avalanche swept debris uncomfortably close to downtown; had the slide fallen even slightly more to the north than it did, the entire community would have been wiped out. As it was, most of the townspeople were unhurt, and there was little or no damage to property.

But not all residents of Frank were so lucky. The landslide completely destroyed two work camps on the lower slopes of Turtle Mountain. No one in either camp stood a chance of surviving the ordeal. Two nearby ranches were demolished by the rocks as well. The force of the landslide killed three men sitting outside the mine entrance and buried all or part of several houses on Alberta Avenue,

The north slope of Turtle Mountain was swept bare of trees and brush after the slide.

on the outskirts of Frank. The total death toll is usually estimated at between seventy and seventy-six, but exact numbers are not available. At least some of the workers killed were transients whose deaths were not reported because their names were not known; and the power of the slide meant that very few bodies were ever recovered.

Still, the disaster did not kill everyone it touched. At the edges of the slide, the rocks had less force behind them and were not piled so high, and survival was a possibility. The landslide wrecked the house of Alberta Avenue

Ben Murgatroyd

As far as is known, only one group of people escaped from the Frank Slide as the rubble came down toward them. That was the crew of a freight train driven by Ben Murgatroyd, an experienced engineer. At 4:00 A.M., Murgatroyd was coasting slowly near the Frank station. He and his crew had just attached several new cars to the engine. As the train moved along, two of the crew members walked alongside the train; it was a bitterly cold night, and they were trying to keep warm.

All at once, Murgatroyd heard an ominous rumbling from above. He decided to take no chances. Quickly he yelled to the men beside the train to climb aboard. Then, as rocks began to fall from the sky, he drove the train forward as fast as it would go. Luckily, the tracks pointed slightly downhill, which gave the train a small extra boost. Perhaps it was the boost that did it; perhaps it was simply Murgatroyd's quick response. But just as the rocks began tumbling onto the tracks, the locomotive pulled beyond the reach of the sliders. Ben Murgatroyd and his crew were safe.

residents Sam and Lucy Ennis, for instance, but the rubble did not rise more than a few feet above the floor. Though trapped beneath fallen beams, Sam Ennis was able to muscle his way out and help Lucy to safety as well. All four Ennis children survived the tragedy, too, including baby Gladys, who was believed to be dead but revived when her mother successfully removed a chunk of earth from her throat.

Another Alberta Avenue survivor was Mrs. John Watkins. The force of the landslide lifted her from her bed and carried her into the nearby Ennis home, the walls of which had been knocked down by the slide. She was flung into the room in which Lucy Ennis's brother, James Warrington, was sleeping. When the Ennises came in to free Warrington, they were shocked to discover Watkins there as well. Watkins was in great distress; as one writer put it, "small splinters of limestone stuck into her body like a pin cushion."[52] But she was alive, and eventually recovered from her wounds.

The Escape of Lester Ackroyd

Probably the most remarkable escape on Alberta Avenue was that of thirteen-year-old Lester Ackroyd, sometimes known as Lester Johnson. The landslide whipped through the home of the teen's family and threw him to the ground. He landed between two huge boulders. The force of the sliding rock tore off his

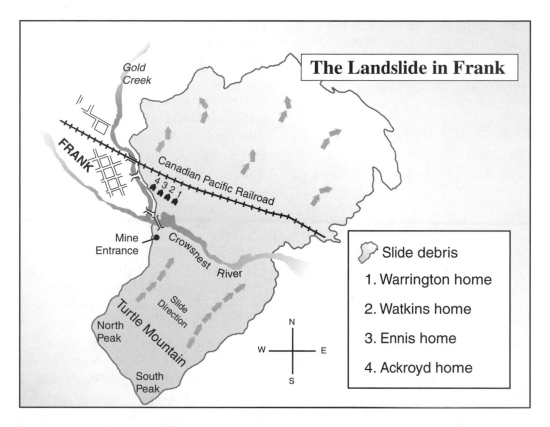

The Landslide in Frank

Gold Creek

FRANK

Canadian Pacific Railroad

4 3 2 1

Mine Entrance

Crowsnest River

Turtle Mountain

Slide Direction

North Peak

South Peak

N
W — E
S

Slide debris
1. Warrington home
2. Watkins home
3. Ennis home
4. Ackroyd home

clothing and drove a sharp fragment of rock deep into his side. The pain was so great that he passed out. But the landslide did not kill him.

Upon regaining consciousness, Ackroyd set out to free himself. First, he pulled out the fragment of rock. The pain in his side was too great to allow him to do anything but crawl, but with great effort he extricated himself from between the boulders. Next, he found a hole between the wreckage of the house and the rocks that had demolished it. Slowly and carefully, Ackroyd made his way through the gap.

He was not yet to safety, however. Alberta Avenue was separated from the main part of town by a creek. Although

there was a bridge across the creek, Ackroyd did not think he had the strength to get there. Instead, he resolved to swim the creek. The water was frigid, he was still naked, and his strength was low. Plunging into the water, he made it safely to the other side and pulled himself ashore. Then he crawled to the nearest house, where the residents were shocked, but delighted, to see that he was alive.

Lester Ackroyd's injuries were serious. The fragment of the rock had gone deep and caused significant damage. The local newspaper reported his wound as a "splinter penetrating [the] liver."[53] Ackroyd needed plenty of medical care and attention. His mother was killed in the disaster; so was his step-father. But he was alive. Through luck and determination, he had escaped their fate.

The Men Underground

The most dramatic escape of all, however, belonged to the seventeen men working the night shift in the mine deep within Turtle Mountain. The men knew exactly when the mountain began to slide. Michael Androz reported later that "the whole mine was [suddenly] pushed together like the bellows of an accordion."[54] Hot air blasted through the corridors. The tunnels began to heave, sending

---

"Frankie Slide"

A number of fanciful legends have sprung up surrounding the landslide at Turtle Mountain. One tale says that a local Native American leader had warned the mayor of Frank to evacuate the community the night before the disaster. Another claims that the town's bank was buried, and with it as much as $500,000 in gold. Neither story is true.

Perhaps the most famous story of the disaster, however, is the tale of Frankie Slide. Supposedly, "Frankie" was a girl about a year and a half old who was found by local residents after her home had been destroyed. She was taken in and cared for; but because no one knew the child's name, she was dubbed "Frankie Slide." Often, the stories insist that Frankie was the only survivor of the catastrophe.

As historian J. William Kerr writes in *Frank Slide,* "They say [Frankie] was found on a rock, on a bale of hay, in her crib, in her attic, on a pile of debris, under the roof of the house, as well as in her dead mother's arms." Over the years the story has grown more and more popular—and more and more fanciful.

In fact, no unknown baby was rescued after the landslide. The tale probably represents a highly imaginative conflation of elements of two true stories. One of the stories was that of Marion Leitch, a small girl who was rescued by neighbors after her parents were killed in the disaster. But the townspeople knew perfectly well who she was. Besides, two of her sisters survived as well, and no one ever called little Marion "Frankie Slide."

The other possible origin of the Frankie Slide story is the true story of Gladys Ennis, the baby whose mother saved her by clearing dirt from her throat. Ennis was saved from the disaster when she was quite young, but there the similarity between her experience and the legend that grew up around "Frankie" ends. Even so, reporters pestered Ennis frequently in attempts to connect her to the mythical Frankie Slide.

A West Virginia coal miner inspects tunnel blockage after the roof of a mine collapsed in 1908. The miners in Turtle Mountain were trapped under 130 feet of rubble.

showers of coal and rock from their ceilings.

The miners had been scattered in different parts of the mine, each intent on his own work assignment. When the landslide struck, however, they immediately made their way to the main entrance. Some moved more quickly than others. Flying debris from the ceiling of a tunnel injured one man's head; another tripped as he ran and hurt his leg. Within a few minutes, though, the shaking had stopped

and the men were gathered at the entrance—which, to their dismay, was completely covered with rubble and rock.

It was clear that a landslide had occurred. The men debated whether it made sense to try to cut their way through the accumulated rubble that blocked their path to freedom. Some of the miners believed that there could be no more than 30 feet of rock between thcm and safety. Others, however, estimated the distance at up to 300 feet. (In

Although the landslide down Turtle Mountain missed the central section of Frank, it destroyed a number of homes and killed approximately seventy-six people.

reality, it was about 130 feet to the outside.) In the end, the men decided that the mouth of the tunnel was too far away. They would look for another way out.

Although the mine had only one main entrance, there were two other potential emergency exits: air shafts, used to ensure a plentiful supply of oxygen inside the mountain. The first was a tunnel carved into the soft stone below the main entrance. This tunnel could be reached through a shaft leading down from the middle of the mountain. The other exit, harder to reach but by no means inaccessible, consisted of two or three shafts that extended above and to the side of the coal deposit. These interconnected shafts all gave access to the outside further up the face of the mountain.

It was of course possible that the landslide had blocked these exits, but on the whole the miners doubted it. Only an exceptionally large landslide could block all three potential escape routes, and they knew such events were quite rare. Leaving the two injured men behind, the rest of the miners hurried down the shaft to the lower level. If the way was clear, they would come back and help their injured comrades to safety.

But the lower tunnel was far from clear. The miners were distressed to find that it was nearly full of water. The landslide had dammed up the Crowsnest River, raising water levels on both sides. River water had crept in steadily through the mouth of the tunnel. There could be no escape this way.

Fear and Terror

Alarmed, the miners returned to the main entrance. Some seized their picks and shovels and attacked the wall of rubble that blocked their path. Three others now made their way up above the coal seam to investigate the upper air shafts. They came back with discouraging news: The shafts were sealed with rock, just as the main entrance was.

This was doubly bad information for the trapped miners. Not only had the slide eliminated the shafts as a possible escape route, but it had also deprived the miners of their source of fresh air. The situation seemed dire. Although the mine was relatively large, the air supply was not infinite. Moreover, the men who had investigated the shafts believed that deadly gas, commonly found in mines, might be building up inside the mine, and with the exits blocked there was no supply of fresh air to flush it out.

The mood turned somber. As Androz put it, the miners began "expecting death [at] any minute."[55] There was nothing to do, it seemed, but to cut their way through the pile of rubble in front of the main entrance. But

as time passed, it became evident that they were making little progress. Clearing heavy limestone was more strenuous and far slower than breaking up the soft coal they were accustomed to handling. "As fast as they dug out rubble," wrote a historian, "more fell into its place."[56]

At some point during the morning of April 29, however, one of the miners had a new idea. He knew that one offshoot of the coal seam led to the surface of the mountain some distance above their heads. Exactly how long this seam was, no one knew; nor did anyone know just where it would come out. There was every chance that this path to freedom would be blocked, too. But at least coal was softer and easier to work with than limestone.

The men agreed to try. They located the offshoot and began to tunnel through the coal. Time was of the essence. They had only a few hours before they would be killed by lethal gases, lack of oxygen, or the rising waters. The seam was so narrow that only two or three men could work on it at once, but the desperate men did their best to remain optimistic. They sang as they worked to keep their spirits up, and they encouraged each other to greater and greater efforts.

But as morning turned to afternoon and they had not broken through, the mood changed once more. Before 5 P.M., the oxygen had dwindled noticeably; every breath became at once more difficult and more precious.

Gradually, the work slowed. The singing stopped. Men sat quietly around the base of the shaft, conserving their energy. Many had given up hope, and some had given up taking their turns in the seam.

To Freedom

Still, a few continued to dig. Among them was Dan McKenzie, one of the men who had made the climb to see whether the air shafts had been blocked; the idea to try escaping through the coal seam may have been his as well, though some sources credit other miners. At about 5:00 in the afternoon, McKenzie thrust his pick up into the air one more time and chopped out another piece of rock. What he saw elated him. As one historian put it, "A beam of brilliant sunshine blinded him and clean air bathed his face."[57]

The discovery energized the rest of the men. They had successfully dug through about thirty feet of coal and limestone in about eight hours. Now they were free. Some sources say that the miners quickly surged through the new tunnel. Others say that falling boulders prevented the men from coming out of this exit, but that they quickly dug another connecting shaft that led to a safer place along the mountainside.

Whatever the final route to the surface, the men soon stood on the ruined hillside in the late afternoon sunshine and gulped in mouthfuls of fresh air. Despite having been trapped deep inside the mountain, they had dug their way to freedom. They had avoided death; they had escaped from the fury of the landslide.

5

Escape from Mount St. Helens

KNOWN FOR THEIR blue lakes and endless evergreen forests, the Cascade Mountains of the Pacific Northwest are widely considered to be among North America's most beautiful mountain ranges. The Cascades are also famous for having some of the tallest and most familiar mountains in the United States. This list includes Mount Rainier, south of Seattle, Washington, which stands over 14,400 feet above sea level; California's Mount Shasta, just a few hundred feet shorter than Rainier; and Mount Hood in northern Oregon.

During the spring of 1980, the attention of the world shifted away from cool mountain lakes and the high peaks of Shasta and Rainier. Instead, the Cascades suddenly became best known for a volcano called Mount St. Helens, located in southwestern Washington about fifty miles northeast of Portland, Oregon. That May, after years of inactivity, Mount St. Helens exploded. The ensuing blast—equivalent to 10 million tons of TNT—destroyed most of the northern side of the mountain and sent a gigantic cloud of ash, smoke, and deadly gas into the atmosphere.

The area immediately surrounding Mount St. Helens was lightly populated, and government officials had done their best to keep people away from the mountain. Still, the eruption threatened thousands of lives. A mass exodus from the region surrounding the mountain ensued, sometimes orderly, more often frantic, as vacationers and townspeople alike hurried to stay ahead of the killer explosion.

St. Helens and Volcanoes

Before 1980, Mount St. Helens had been a dormant, or inactive, volcano for over a century. In geological terms, however, its volcanic activity had been quite recent. As late as 1842, an eyewitness described "vast columns of lurid smoke and fire"[58] pouring out the top of St. Helens. And twentieth-century scientists realized that St. Helens had been exceptionally active during the preceding few thousand years. The mountain's history seemed to make it a good candidate to erupt again. In 1975, in fact, one study predicted that St. Helens would explode within the next twenty-five years.

Few people outside the scientific community paid much attention to this prediction, however. To most people, St. Helens was first and foremost a beautiful mountain. The wilderness around St. Helens attracted campers looking for a quiet spot to spend a week or two. The forests held birds, deer, and other wildlife. Some people built vacation homes along nearby Spirit Lake, and the YMCA and the Boy Scouts constructed camps within sight of the peak. It was hard to think of such a pretty mountain as a dangerous volcano.

Early in 1980, however, the situation changed dramatically. The first signs of danger were small earthquakes in the area late in March. These disturbances suggested that some kind of activity

was going on inside the mountain. Within a week, the top of the mountain had begun to release ash and hot gases. Scientists, reporters, and tourists flocked to the peak. Excitement was high: St. Helens was the first volcano to erupt in the forty-eight contiguous states since 1921, when California's Mount Lassen—also in the Cascades—had gone dormant after eight years of activity.

For nearly two months, St. Helens put on a regular show for those who watched. Minor eruptions sent more steam and ash into the sky. A small crater developed on one side of the mountain. Local residents sold T-shirts and other lighthearted souvenirs of the volcano.

However, scientists knew that the situation was more serious than most members of the public believed. There was no guarantee that St. Helens would continue to vent in relatively harmless ways. On the contrary, the small eruptions were a sign that a big explosion was on its way—and the consequences of such a blast could be devastating.

Limiting Access

On the advice of the volcano specialists, state authorities took steps to protect people from a possible major eruption. Washington governor Dixy Lee Ray established a "red zone" extending five miles in each direction from the mountain's peak. Other than law enforcement officials and scientists, no one was allowed in this area.

A pedestrian, seen through a car's windshield, walks through an empty town covered in ash after the eruption of Mount St. Helens.

Those living next to Spirit Lake were evacuated, and visitors to the region were told to stay away.

Ray also set up a "blue zone" just outside the boundaries of the red zone. This area was less restricted than the red zone, but permits were required for entry, and no one was allowed to spend the night. And even beyond the blue zone, government officials urged residents and travelers to take note of potential evacuation routes.

However, not everyone was willing to follow the governor's orders. Some tourists, for example, were unwilling to experience the volcano from behind roadblocks. Some drove right by security officers at barricades. Others used obscure logging roads to evade the authorities. Guards were able to keep some of these overly zealous travelers away, but they could not stop them all.

Nor were local residents any more eager to support the restrictions on access. The evacuated homeowners were particularly upset. As April wore on and the volcano did not erupt, they began to press government officials to lift the restrictions. Local merchants worried that roadblocks would cut into their business; logging companies lobbied to increase their access to the blue zone. And those who lived farther away relaxed as time passed. Perhaps, they thought, the mountain would not explode after all.

Volcanic Dangers

In truth, the boundaries of the red and blue zones probably should have been extended outward. Scientists knew that any large blast would certainly affect areas well beyond the specified danger zone. Ideally, people would have been evacuated from communities many miles past the blue zone's border. For political reasons, however, this was not to be. It was hard enough to convince those nearest the volcano of the dan-

gers. Hoping to forestall further complaints, state officials made the danger zones as small as possible.

Indeed, political pressure occasionally caused Washington State officials to ignore scientific advice altogether. A few roadblocks were actually moved closer to the mountain to allow easier access to certain stores and businesses. Similarly, logging companies persuaded officials to leave open an area near the western slope of St. Helens. And on May 17, state employees allowed Spirit Lake homeowners to return briefly to the area to collect valuables. "It was clearly pointed out that [the return] was considered to be too great a risk,"[59] remembered a scientist

Mount St. Helens was dormant for over a century before it erupted in 1980. It was the first volcano to erupt in the continental United States since 1921.

who worked with the U.S. Geological Service. Nevertheless, state leaders permitted the trip.

To residents and officials, though, the benefits of allowing people near the volcano seemed to outweigh the risks. The truth was that no one knew when— or even whether—St. Helens would stage a major eruption. Even the most experienced scientists have trouble making clear predictions about volcanic explosions. It is impossible to foresee the hour, the day, or even the month of an upcoming eruption, and equally impossible to determine how serious that eruption will be. With the timing and effects of an explosion uncertain, the people and leaders of Washington were willing to take a few chances.

Although no one knew exactly what would happen, scientists were aware that eruptions had the power to kill. Lava, or molten rock from the inside of the volcano, can flow down the slopes of a mountain during an eruption. Volcanic explosions may release super-heated gases, which can burn people to death many miles from the site of the blast. Ashes can be dangerous, too. Depending on the direction and strength of the wind, ash from a volcanic eruption may be thick enough to suffocate those unable to escape.

The circumstances of St. Helens made several other dangers possible, too. Explosions can send pieces of lava flying in a so-called blast cloud, destroying every living thing for miles; several scientists thought St. Helens was likely to explode in this way.

Moreover, the slopes of the mountain had become unstable. Scientists feared landslides and mudflows if the mountain should erupt. These slides would surely move faster than a person could run, and possibly faster than a car could travel. They could also fill in surrounding rivers and lakes, presenting hazards downstream.

But while scientists knew of these issues, they had trouble explaining them to the public. In part, this was because scientists are trained to speak in probabilities and hypotheticals. Rather than describing in detail what they expected to happen, they talked about what *might* take place or what the effects *could* be. The result was that local residents, tourists, and even some government officials never really grasped the hazards.

The problem also lay with human nature. "Even if they live at the foot of a volcano," comments writer Alwyn Scarth, "[people] find it hard to imagine incandescent clouds of ash careering down their [Main] Street at 500 km an hour."[60] St. Helens had never exploded within living memory. Nor had any other U.S. mountain outside Alaska or Hawaii. Despite the warnings, it seemed inconceivable to many that anything truly disastrous could take place.

The Mountain Erupts

On Sunday morning, May 18, there was very little activity near St. Helens. The weekend and early hours had cut down on the number of loggers in the area, and the blue and red zones were virtually empty but for scientists and a few people camping illegally. Many others, however, though outside the blue zone, were close enough to the mountain to see it clearly. That group included campers, anglers, and others on the banks of the nearby Toutle River and in the forests a dozen or more miles from the volcano.

At 8:32 that morning, another small earthquake rattled the area. As geologists later reconstructed the chain of events, the quake shook the top of the volcano, sending a small landslide of debris down the mountain's northern slope. The movement of rock and ice downhill reduced some of the pressure that had been keeping gases and hot lava inside the mountain. Given space to expand, steam and molten rock cascaded out of the volcano. The eruption had begun.

To those who saw it, the explosion was remarkable. "We were greeted by a sight that looked like [movie director] Cecil B. DeMille's *The Ten Commandments,*" recalled Robert Barrett, who saw the blast from a nearby lake. "Blue, black and purple smoke spewed from the top of the mountain while jagged yellow flashes of lightning streaked from the smoke and pierced the ground."[61] Photographs taken by eyewitnesses show ash soaring from the crater as rock and debris tumble down the side. Television broadcasters groped

A Short-Lived Sense of Disappointment

At the time of the explosion, Keith and Dorothy Stoffel were flying over the top of Mount St. Helens in a chartered airplane. The two were geologists, monitoring the volcano's progress from the sky. As quoted by Neil Modie in "Memories of Awesome Power, Silent Fury," Keith Stoffel remembered looking down in the first few minutes of the flight and feeling "a sense of disappointment that nothing was happening."

Less than an hour later, Stoffel's sense of disappointment would vanish quickly and dramatically. As the Stoffels and the pilot watched from above, Mount St. Helens exploded. Excited and awed as the Stoffels were, they had other things to think about: The small airplane was right in the path of the deadly cloud.

The plane's pilot responded immediately. "The pilot opened full throttle and dove quickly to gain speed," the Stoffels recalled, as quoted in Alwyn Scarth, *Vulcan's Fury.* "The cloud behind us was mushrooming to unbelievable dimensions and appeared to be catching up with us." But the plane could fly in any direction, and the pilot quickly figured out which way to go. Because the clouds were moving north, he turned the plane south. Avoiding the worst of the blast, the three landed a few minutes later at the airport in Portland, Oregon.

Mount St. Helens erupts, spewing ash and debris into the sky. The explosion was worse than scientists anticipated.

for words to describe the drama of the blast.

In many ways, the explosion of St. Helens was worse than most scientists had anticipated. The explosion tore off one side of the mountain, leaving a gaping hole. Lava from deep inside St. Helens catapulted into the atmosphere, along with two cubic miles of rocks, ice, trees, and other materials from the surface. Boulders, molten rock, and pieces of stone and ice smashed into the surrounding forest.

Traveling with them were gases released by the explosion. Scientists later estimated that these poisonous vapors traveled outward from the volcano at nearly the speed of sound. Heated to about 1300°F, the gases killed every living thing they encountered within several miles of the blast site. The combination of flying particles and deadly gas most seriously affected a zone of two hundred square miles next to one side of the mountain. Within this area, destruction was total.

Flying debris was not the only problem. Much of the rock, lava, and other material on top of St. Helens simply slid down the slope. This burden gathered speed until it was traveling at a rate estimated at nearly two hundred miles per hour. The slide stripped the lower slopes of the mountain of vegetation; then the rocks and other debris tumbled across the countryside. In an instant, every house along Spirit Lake had been destroyed, and the bottom of the lake itself had been filled to a depth of nearly two hundred feet.

At almost the same time, hot, thick ash began to fall from the sky—volcanic material that had been sent eighty thousand feet into the atmosphere during the eruption was now settling back to earth. All around the mountain, the ash was so thick that seeing was almost impossible. "It's dark as hell," reported the director of a nearby environmental camp an hour after the explosion. "We have two inches of ash on the ground."[62] The situation, of course, was far worse closer to the blast site.

The Escape Begins

Despite the devastation caused by the eruption, however, the death toll from Mount St. Helens was relatively small. Of the fifty-seven people known to have died in the blast, those who had been in the area most affected had had no possibility of escape. Gerald Martin, for instance, was on a ridge just outside the red zone that morning, helping to monitor the volcano's progress. In a radio transmission, he described how the cloud of hot ash covered a nearby car. "It is going to get me too,"[63] he said just before he died.

Still, the death toll could have been far higher. The extent and fury of the eruption caught almost everyone by surprise. Campers and local residents who thought they were a safe distance from the volcano were horrified to find that they were not. Most in this position did not simply give in to death; instead, they tried to escape it. A few people died trying to outrun the cloud of ash, or were unable to find refuge from the landslides. But the great majority succeeded in escaping the eruption's disastrous effects.

How those who fled carried out their escapes depended on where they were and on the means available to them. Some had cars at their disposal. Others had to rely on their legs and their own ingenuity. Similarly, some who escaped were able to reach safety on their own, while others could only put themselves in a place from which they could be rescued. The eruption did not treat all the people equally.

There was one important similarity among the escapes, however: a delayed reaction to the danger. Most of those who escaped had thought at first that they were safe from the eruption. Trixie Anders, for example, watched the explosion with her husband and two other men from a ridge several miles beyond the danger zone. The three men wanted to stay and watch the drama unfold in front of them. Anders was tempted, too, but fortunately, she was a geologist by training. Recognizing the seriousness of the situation, she practically forced the men to evacuate—scant minutes before the deadly cloud of gas and debris rolled in.

With hindsight, it appears that those who were closer to the blast site should have been more aware of the dangers. A surprising number of these people

Anatomy of the Mount St. Helens Eruption

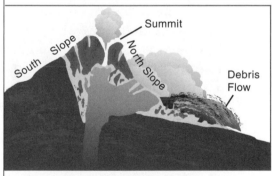

May 18, 1980, 8:32 A.M.: An earthquake shook material loose from the north slope, causing a landslide.

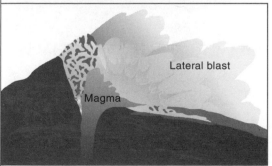

The landslide relieved the pressure on the gas and lava, triggering a lateral blast, which tore off the north slope.

Ash covers a pickup truck. The eruption released tons of ash into the air that fell back onto Washington State.

people most in need of a quick escape route.

The absence of sound played a role, too. Hundreds of miles away in northern Montana, the explosion sounded like cannon fire—but because of the heavy ash and the path taken by the sound waves, the eruption was completely inaudible to most people near Mount St. Helens. The noise made by a blast might have spurred people to evacuate more quickly. The lack of any sound, in contrast, tended to diminish the apparent threat.

And some people were mesmerized by the power and majesty of the exploding mountain. Many of the onlookers were aware that they were witnessing history. Some took the time to marvel at the spectacle before deciding to flee. "We didn't know whether to take more pictures," recalled Darren Greenwood of Kelso, Washington, who observed the eruption with his cousin, "or get the hell out of there."[65] In the end, the men snapped a few extra shots before hurrying away at top speed. Many others would do the same.

"An Earthquake Inside You"

The most remarkable escapes from the fury of Mount St. Helens were made by people camping near the blast site. The eruption put these survivors in grave peril. Most were in remote areas

did not immediately head for cover. Local residents, in particular, had been lulled by nearly two months of constant warnings without a major explosion. "They talked about it blowing up, but nobody believed it,"[64] recalled Buzz Smith, who was camping with his two sons near the blue zone. This skepticism initially slowed some of the distant from roads, which made it hard to find an escape route. They also had to deal with several aspects of the volcano at once. The hot ash, the poisonous gases, and the ravaging effects of the landslides worked together to make escape extremely difficult—but absolutely essential.

Despite their initial confusion about the size and impact of the blast, most of the nearby campers realized the dangers soon enough. Many signs were unmistakable. Buzz Smith, for instance, knew it was time to react when stones the size of golf balls began falling from the sky. Another camper, Lu heard a rumbling sound in the her family's campsite about twelve miles north of the volcano. "It felt like there was an earthquake inside you,"[66] she recalled afterward.

A third survivor, nineteen-year-old Roald Reitan, was camping beside the Toutle River when St. Helens erupted. Reitan's first indication that something was wrong was a sudden series of changes in the river. As debris tumbled into the river further upstream, Reitan noticed the river beginning to rise. Twigs, leaves, and branches filled the

Flying Ash

Most of the effects of the eruption were confined to the area immediately around Mount St. Helens. The major exception was the ashfall. Winds picked up 520 million tons of fine gray ash and carried the flakes in several different directions. Ashes fell lightly on Portland, Oregon, to the south of St. Helens; on Seattle, Washington, to the north; and on many other communities in between.

But the prevailing winds were from the west, and so the ashes fell most heavily to the east. Much of eastern Washington was buried in gritty, powdery ash; some towns were covered in six inches of it. Ash stalled the engines of cars and choked air conditioners. Authorities cautioned people to stay indoors and to wear surgical masks whenever possible.

Weddings were postponed; schools were closed; businesses shut down to enable employees to spend their time cleaning up. In some places, it took months to remove all the ashes.

Past eastern Washington, the ashfall diminished. The ash cloud spread across much of the northern United States, but little of it settled; most people would not have noticed a change if they had not known about the eruption. Nevertheless, the ashes were strong enough to affect weather patterns. Three days after the eruption, the ash cloud crossed Washington, D.C. Twelve days after that, scientists could still recognize it as it swept once more across the Mount St. Helens area. In fifteen days, the ashes had circled the globe.

current, and the normally clear waters darkened and thickened until, in Reitan's words, the river looked like "chocolate pudding."[67] Reitan had heard and felt nothing, but the Toutle's behavior told him that he was in serious danger.

But no matter how quickly they recognized the danger, the speed and destructiveness of the eruption left most of the campers with few options. Smith, for instance, knew that he and his sons could not outrun the flurry of rocks and the ash that would descend just a few moments later. Instead, the three took refuge under a cedar tree. Smith spread their sleeping bags over a branch to serve as a makeshift shelter. Then he and his sons huddled beneath the branch.

Lu Moore's family was only slightly better off. Grabbing as many of their belongings as they could, Moore, her husband, and their two young daughters headed down the trail to a shelter sometimes used by hunters. But particles of the hot ash penetrated the roof and sides of the shelter, contaminating the air. The Moores had the presence of mind to breathe through socks, which saved them from choking on the ash.

While far from perfect, the shelters used by the Moores and the Smiths did help shield those survivors from the most deadly effects of the explosion. "I remember thinking, 'This has got to be like hell,'"[68] Smith reported years later, recalling the hot ash falling all around them. Still, like the Moores, Smith and his sons were relatively fortunate.

Without the shelters, they would surely have perished. Once the effects of the eruption had subsided, both families were spotted by rescue helicopters and airlifted to safety.

Escape from the Green River

Other campers in the area made different choices. The night before the blast, Bruce Nelson and Sue Ruff were camping with friends along the Green River north of St. Helens. Because of wind conditions and other environmental factors, the effects of the explosion hit their campground particularly dramatically. Within moments of the blast, the whole area was covered with heated ash, falling trees, and rocks. Across most of the campground, the debris quickly reached a depth of eight feet.

Unlike the Smiths and the Moores, Nelson and Ruff were still in their tent when the volcano blew up. As the ash and debris settled around them, burying their tent deep beneath the surface, they immediately set to work digging their way out. This was a terrifying experience, and the ash was so hot that it singed their flesh as they dug. To stay in the tent, however, would have meant death by suffocation.

Reaching the surface was no guarantee of safety. When Nelson and Ruff emerged, they were met with more ash falling heavily from the sky. "It was like someone pouring a bag of it over your head,"[69] one survivor recalled later. Indeed, the ash was so thick they had

Trucks remain buried under ash and felled trees. Some who stayed in the area too long after the eruption were killed by the suffocating ash.

to use their fingers to scoop it out of their mouths. And the ash was not the only problem: The air was also filled with flying rocks and pieces of ice from the glaciers on top of the mountain.

Nelson and Ruff decided that their best chances for survival lay in seeking refuge farther from the blast site. First, though, they took a few minutes to check on their friends. Two did not respond to their repeated cries; searchers later found that falling debris had killed them. Dan Balch and Bryan Thomas, however, were still alive and quickly joined Nelson and Ruff.

Thomas had suffered a broken hip in the explosion. At first the other three

thought they might be able to carry him to safety, but Thomas proved too heavy. Instead, Balch, Ruff, and Nelson joined forces to build their friend a makeshift shelter. They set up a barrier of logs and maneuvered Thomas behind them. "It was a hard thing to do," Nelson recalled later. "Bryan was screaming, 'Don't leave me here! Don't leave me here to die!'"[70] But the other three felt they had little choice. They left Thomas behind, promising to return with help as soon as they could.

Next the group headed out across the ash. This time it was Balch who suffered most. He was barefoot, and the heated ash severely burned his feet. Before long, he elected to stay behind.

Nelson and Ruff kept going, dodging falling rocks and trees that blocked their path. A few miles farther on, they encountered another camper who had survived the explosion. Here they stopped; conditions were better than they had been at the Green River campground. Later that day, they signaled a rescue helicopter and were picked up. Balch and Thomas were flown to safety as well.

Fleeing the Toutle

An even more dramatic escape was carried out by Roald Reitan, the young man encamped by the Toutle River, and his girlfriend, Venus Ann Dergan. It was the sight of the swollen, dirt-choked river that persuaded them to leave the area. But in the time it took the pair to reach their car, the rising waters of the Toutle had encircled them. Reitan and Dergan clambered onto the roof of the car, hoping to stay away from the churning waters; but even that was no refuge.

Within minutes the violent current threatened to tear Reitan and Dergan off the roof of the car and sweep them downstream. Instead, the two jumped onto a pile of floating logs the landslide had wrenched from the hillsides. "On the surface," Reitan remembered, "the big logs looked like a raft."[71] Underneath, however, smaller logs were churning furiously, sucking the upper logs down. Reitan managed to keep his head above the water, though the pounding of the logs injured his leg.

Damage from St. Helens was widespread. The eruption triggered huge landslides and flooding.

Dergan, less robust, slipped beneath the surface. At first Reitan was sure she had drowned, but then he saw her hand sticking above the roaring waters. He tried to pull her up, only to watch the waters seize her again. The next time Reitan caught a glimpse of her, he grabbed her by the hair to get her head above the water.

The two rode the logs downstream for about ten minutes. The experience, Reitan recalled later, was "like being in a washing machine full of mud, logs and rocks."[72] Eventually the current subsided somewhat, and Reitan and Dergan were able to wade ashore at a point approximately three miles from where they had started. Despite their injuries, the two had the strength to dash to a nearby hill, away from the floodwaters. There they waited until a rescue helicopter arrived to carry them to safety.

Escape by Car

Not all the escapes from Mount St. Helens were made on foot—or by river. Many people escaped the volcano by driving away from it at speeds ranging up to one hundred miles an hour. To be sure, this breakneck pace put the cars in danger of crashing. But the alternative was that the driver and passengers would be overtaken by the effects of the volcano—and in all likelihood, killed.

Among those who escaped by car was Trixie Anders, the geologist who had been watching the blast from a distant ridge. She and her husband left their vantage point as soon as she saw the cloud of ash and fiery gas advancing toward them. The two drove away from the blast at top speed, barely paying attention to the twists and turns in the road. "We careened around the curves on two tires," Anders wrote later. "I truly believed that we would not survive."[73] Fifteen agonizing minutes passed before they knew they had outrun the volcano.

At Bear Meadow, just outside the restricted zone, camper Keith Ronnholm had a similar experience. He had delayed his escape to take photographs of the eruption. The decision almost cost him his life. On the drive out, the edge of the blast overtook him. Heavy ash pelted down out of the sky, and even with his headlights on Ronnholm could scarcely see a yard in front of him. In the darkness, he escaped the area only by creeping along as fast as he dared, following the taillights of a logging truck which in turn was being led by men on foot.

Some combined escape by vehicle with escape on foot. Television cameraman Dave Crockett was not far from the west slope of the mountain early the morning of the eruption. When the mountain blew up, he hurried back to his car and floored the gas pedal, intending to return to the main highway. But as he approached a deep gully along the way, a wall of mud and branches swept away the only bridge that crossed it.

Crockett screeched to a halt just before hitting the debris head-on. He threw the car into reverse, hoping to

"I Couldn't Tell Where the Road Was"

Even far from the volcano, many people had to escape from the flying ash. "Darkness descended on us with a fury," recalled Roberta Dickerson, who was on a highway over a hundred miles from the volcano when the cloud reached her. "Wind-whipped ash filled the air . . . I couldn't tell where the road was." Dickerson eventually was forced to stop by the side of the highway until conditions improved slightly. Her account can be found on the Internet at www.mtsthelens.net.

Even then, Dickerson was uncertain how long she could survive breathing the ash-choked air. To reach safety, Dickerson joined forces with other drivers in the vicinity who had also stopped. Setting their cars nearly bumper to bumper, they drove as a caravan through the swirling ash, each following the car in front as closely as possible. Their average speed was under ten miles an hour, but anything faster would have put them in danger of driving off the road. After a harrowing drive, the group finally came to a restaurant, where they took refuge until the worst of the ashfall was over.

a logging road. He was rescued by helicopters later that afternoon.

Success

Hazardous as the escapes by air, by foot and by water were, most were ultimately successful. In fact, nearly all the people near Mount St. Helens that day survived the blast. Despite the ash, the gases, the landslides, and the other potentially deadly effects of the volcanic eruption, very few people were killed. In part, the low death toll was due to the quick response by emergency teams, which sent out helicopters as soon as possible to look for survivors.

Credit, however, also goes to those who survived. Whether they escaped the blast by driving their cars at breakneck speeds along the highways, riding logs down the Toutle River, or finding or constructing the best possible shelter, those who fled from death had kept themselves alive under difficult circumstances. Their escapes were dramatic, courageous—and most important of all, successful.

escape by going back into the forest. But that was impossible; almost everything behind him had been destroyed. Instead, Crockett left the car and headed up a nearby ridge. For over an hour he wandered in the darkness, until the ash cleared enough for him to find

Appendix

Documents Pertaining to Natural Disasters

Pliny and the Eruption of Vesuvius

The Roman historian and writer Pliny the Younger was a witness to the eruption of Mount Vesuvius in A.D. 79. When the volcano exploded, he was in the town of Misenum on the Bay of Naples in present-day Italy. Pliny's uncle, known as Pliny the Elder, had gone closer to the volcano and was missing when it erupted. Pliny the Younger hesitated to leave the area, hoping to find his uncle, but ultimately gave up the search; it later turned out that Pliny the Elder had died during the disaster.

In this excerpt, Pliny the Younger explains how he, his mother, and several others managed to escape the effects of the volcano. The "cloud" he refers to is the cloud of ash and rock released into the atmosphere by the explosion.

That night the shaking grew much stronger; people thought it was an upheaval, not just a tremor. My mother burst into my room and I got up. I said she should rest, and I would rouse her. . . . We sat out on a small terrace between the house and the sea. I sent for a volume of Livy [a Roman writer], I read and even took notes from where I had left off, as if it were a moment of free time; I hardly know whether to call it bravery, or foolhardiness (I was seventeen at the time). Up comes a friend of my uncle's, recently arrived from Spain. When he sees my mother and me sitting there, and me even reading a book, he scolds her for her calm and me for my lack of concern. But I kept on with my book.

Now the day begins, with a still hesitant and almost lazy dawn. All around us buildings are shaken. We are in the open, but it is only a small area and we are afraid, nay certain, that there will be a collapse. We decided to leave the town finally; a dazed crowd follows us, preferring our plan to their own (this is what passes for wisdom in a panic). Their numbers are so large that they slow our departure, and then sweep us along. We stopped once we had left the buildings behind us. Many strange things happened to us there, and we had much to fear.

The carts that we had ordered brought were moving in opposite directions, though the ground was perfectly flat, and they wouldn't stay in place even with their wheels blocked by stones. In addition, it seemed as though the sea was being sucked backwards, as if it were being pushed back by the shaking of the land. Certainly the shoreline moved outwards, and many sea creatures were left on dry sand. Behind us were frightening dark clouds, rent by lightning twisted and hurled, opening to reveal huge figures of flame. These were like lightning, but bigger. At that point the Spanish friend urged us strongly: "If your brother and uncle is alive, he wants you to be safe. If he has perished, he wanted you to survive him. So why are you reluctant to escape?" We responded that we would not look to our own safety as long as we were uncertain about his. Waiting no longer, he took himself off from the danger at a mad pace. It wasn't long thereafter that the cloud stretched down to the ground and covered the sea. It girdled Capri [an island] and made it vanish, it hid Misenum's promontory [peninsula]. Then my mother began to beg and urge and order me to flee however I might, saying that a young man could make it, that she, weighed down in years and body, would die happy if she escaped being the cause of my death. I replied that I wouldn't save myself without her, and then I took her hand and made her walk a little faster. She obeyed with difficulty, and blamed herself for delaying me.

Now came the dust, though still thinly. I look back: a dense cloud looms behind us, following us like a flood poured across the land. "Let us turn aside while we can still see, lest we be knocked over in the street and crushed by the crowd of our companions." We had scarcely sat down when a darkness came that was not like a moonless or cloudy night, but more like the black of closed and unlighted rooms. You could hear women lamenting, children crying, men shouting. Some were calling for parents, others for children or spouses; they could only recognize them by their voices. Some bemoaned their own lot, other that of their near and dear. There were some so afraid of death that they prayed for death. Many raised their hands to the gods, and even more believed that there were no gods any longer and that this was one last unending night for the world. Nor were we without people who magnified real dangers with fictitious horrors. Some announced that one or another part of Misenum had collapsed or burned; lies, but they found believers. It grew lighter, though that seemed not a return of day, but a sign that the fire was approaching. The fire itself actually stopped some distance away, but darkness and ashes came again, a great weight of them. We stood up and shook the ash off again and again, otherwise we would have been covered with it and crushed by the weight. I might boast that no groan escaped me in such perils, no cowardly word, but that I believed that I was perishing with the world, and the world with me, which was a great consolation for death.

At last the cloud thinned out and dwindled to no more than smoke or fog. Soon there was real daylight. The sun was even shining, though with the lurid glow it has after an eclipse. The sight that met our still terrified eyes was a changed world, buried in ash like snow. We returned to Misenum and took care of our bodily needs, but spent the night dangling between hope and fear. Fear was the stronger, for the earth was still quaking and a number of people who had gone mad were mocking the evils that had happened to them and others with terrifying prognostications [predictions]. We still refused to go until we heard news of my uncle, although we had felt danger and expected more.

Pliny Letter VI.20.

Saved from a Tornado

On March 3, 1966, a devastating tornado hit Jackson, Mississippi. The storm killed fourteen people and leveled large swaths of the city. Among the people who escaped were Donna Durr, a teacher, and her two-year-old son Derryl, who were driving home from a shopping trip when the tornado struck. The excerpt comes from Lorian Hemingway's A World Turned Over, *a book about the disaster; Hemingway was a young woman living in Jackson at the time of the storm.*

It is a happening rare even in the bizarre files of freak tornado experiences, rare in that those who feel the crushing pressure and high-velocity winds of the storm's interior ever live to tell about it, rarer still that they are conscious when it happens. The little green Volkswagen began to rise into the air with Donna Durr still at the wheel, her child beside her.

"We just started being lifted up," she remembers, her voice still filled with wonder more than thirty years later. "We were just lifted and we were bouncing, and you know, all this sounds so crazy, the more I think about it, the more I tell it, just asking the *whys* of it. *Why* weren't we blown with the rest of what was blown away, and *why* didn't we swirl? We bounced and bounced and got lifted higher and higher."

Once they were deep within the vortex, the assault by the debris became constant. Her little boy began to cry and then to scream. Donna Durr pulled her son to her and lay his head in her lap, she says, "to shield his little face and eyes and all." She thought then about her own eyes, of the hard contact lenses she was wearing, and whether she might be blinded. And they rose still higher, seventy-five feet straight up, a man who had been watching on the ground, watching from afar, would later say, above the tops of the old oaks and the sycamores, far beyond the telephone wires that were being stripped from their moorings. And then Donna Durr dared to look down.

"It was like I was in a cartoon," she says. "I was just way, way up there in the air looking down, and Derryl was just screaming, and then all of a sudden we were right by the two-story electric power building, and I saw that thing just explode. It looked like you would have a little toy block house on the floor and just kicked it. Bricks went everywhere."

The explosion of bricks that blew out from the power substation heralded the hour and the minute that the clocks stopped in South Jackson and all fell into darkness. As Donna Durr watched the airborne bricks being sucked deep into the center where she still rode high, she says that there was one phrase, and one phrase only, in her mind. "I thought, 'Oh, no, *this is it.*'" She says she thought there would be some rush of wisdom that would form itself in her mind and offer up, perhaps, a Bible verse or the words of a philosopher or her own words that spoke of who she had been, and what her life had meant, but there it was—*this is it*—unadorned, brutal almost, the most succinct euphemism for a life about to be taken, when you hadn't had time to prepare for it at all. But instead of the knowledge that she hoped would fill her, what she felt was peace, she says, and she still cannot explain the depth of it or how suddenly it visited her while she was rising above the parking lot of Candlestick [shopping center], all the cars below her destroyed in a heap of tortured metal and busted-out glass.

"I wasn't even thinking about dying and going to Heaven," she says, "and I wasn't callin' out to Jesus. I wasn't. I don't know why." Perhaps, she thought, because Jesus most likely knew. "Those are the kinds of questions I'm still asking myself now, why didn't I call out, other than, I guess, I just had a peace that He was in control, even though I wasn't consciously saying it."

And at the moment that she became conscious of that unbidden peace, with the remnants of houses and the power station bricks and the pieces of Candlestick Park hitting the car from all sides, Donna Durr and her small son began to descend through the cloud.

"About that time, as I felt this, we just started comin' down, just as gently as we went up, and that tornado blew every brick off that concrete foundation of the power station. There was not a brick left. It was like you had taken a broom and just swept it off. The Lord just put us right back down. I mean, just as gently as you would put a toy car on the floor. The only way I can visualize it is that the Lord just picked us up and blew that thing right under us, and set us right back down. And when I got out, once I realized we were down, I picked my baby up and I just stood there and looked. By that time it was just pouring torrents of rain, you could hardly even see. But I looked around and the whole shopping center was flat. And there was not a person moving. Not one."

Lorian Hemingway, *A World Turned Over,* 2002.

Notes

Chapter One: Escape from the Johnstown Flood

1. Quoted in *Wild Weather.* Danbury, CT: Grolier, 1998, p. 14.
2. Quoted in David G. McCullough, *The Johnstown Flood.* New York: Simon & Schuster, 1968, p. 88.
3. Victor Heiser, *An American Doctor's Odyssey.* New York: W.W. Norton, 1936, p. 3.
4. Quoted in "The Day the Dam Broke," *Reader's Digest,* May 1989, p. 201.
5. Quoted in McCullough, *The Johnstown Flood,* p. 100.
6. Quoted in *Wild Weather,* p. 13.
7. Heiser, *An American Doctor's Odyssey,* p. 4.
8. Quoted in Donald Dale Jackson, "When 20 Million Tons of Water Flooded Johnstown," *Smithsonian,* May 1989, p. 54.
9. Quoted in McCullough, *The Johnstown Flood,* p. 116.
10. Quoted in McCullough, *The Johnstown Flood,* p. 120.
11. Quoted in McCullough, *The Johnstown Flood*, p. 121.
12. Heiser, *An American Doctor's Odyssey,* p. 4.
13. Heiser, *An American Doctor's Odyssey,* p. 4.
14. Heiser, *An American Doctor's Odyssey,* p. 5.
15. Quoted in McCullough, *The Johnstown Flood,* p. 162.
16. Quoted in Hal Butler, *Nature at War.* Chicago: Henry Regnery, 1976, p. 170.
17. Quoted in Edwin Hutcheson, "A Brief History of the 1889 Johnstown Flood." www.jaha.org.

Chapter Two: The Armenian Earthquake

18. Quoted in "Vision of Horror," *Time,* December 26, 1988, p. 33.
19. Quoted in Yuri Rost, *Armenian Tragedy,* trans. Elizabeth Roberts. New York: St. Martin's Press, 1990, p. 2.
20. Quoted in "The 1988 Armenian Earthquake." www.clarkhumanities. org.
21. Quoted in "Sorrow Felt Around World," *USA Today,* December 13,

1988, p. 6A.

22. Quoted in "When the Earth Shook," *Time*, December 19, 1988, p. 34.
23. Quoted in "Lived Through the 1988 Tragedy." www.clarkhumanities.org.
24. Quoted in "Lived Through the 1988 Tragedy," www.clarkhumanities.org.
25. Quoted in "Leninakan's Earthquake—Maro Gharibyan." www.clarkhumanities.org.
26. Quoted in Rost, *Armenian Tragedy*, p. 2.

Chapter Three: The Fire at Storm King

27. Quoted in Sebastian Junger, *Fire*. New York: W.W. Norton, 2001, p. 39.
28. Bill Donahue et al., "Tragedy at Storm King," *American Forests,* January 1995, p. 17+.
29. Quoted in Junger, *Fire*, p. 46.
30. Quoted in John N. Maclean, *Fire on the Mountain*. New York: William Morrow, 1999, p. 75.
31. Quoted in "To Be Young Once, and Brave," *Time*, July 18, 1994, p. 32+.
32. Quoted in Robert Davis et al., "Back into the 'Black,'" *USA Today,* July 8, 1994, p. 3A+.
33. Quoted in Davis, "Back into the 'Black,'" p. 3A+.
34. Quoted in Maclean, *Fire on the Mountain,* p. 127.
35. Quoted in Junger, *Fire*, p. 48.
36. Quoted in Maclean, *Fire on the Mountain,* p. 135.
37. Quoted in Junger, *Fire*, p. 48.
38. Quoted in Junger, *Fire*, p. 50.
39. Quoted in Donahue et al., "Tragedy at Storm King," p. 17+.
40. Quoted in Maclean, *Fire on the Mountain,* p. 145.
41. Quoted in Donahue et al., "Tragedy at Storm King," p. 17+.
42. Quoted in Maclean, *Fire on the Mountain,* p. 145.
43. Quoted in Donahue et al., "Tragedy at Storm King," p. 17+.
44. Quoted in Donahue et al., "Tragedy at Storm King," p. 17+.

Chapter Four: Escape from the Frank Landslide

45. Quoted in J. William Kerr, *Frank Slide*. Calgary, Alberta, Canada: Barker, 1990, p. 3.
46. Quoted in Allen Seager, "Frank Slide," *Beaver*, April/May 1996, no page given.
47. Kerr, *Frank Slide,* p. 5.
48. Quoted in Seager, "Frank Slide," no page given.
49. Quoted in *Tragedies of the Crowsnest Pass*. Surrey, British Columbia, Canada: Heritage House, 1983, p. 43.
50. Kerr, *Frank Slide,* p. 6.
51. Quoted in *Tragedies of the Crowsnest Pass,* p. 27.
52. "Frank Slide, Alberta: The Day the Mountain Fell." www.sympatico.ca.
53. Quoted in Kerr, *Frank Slide,* p. 21.
54. Quoted in Seager, *Frank Slide,* no page given.
55. Quoted in Seager, *Frank Slide,* no page given.
56. "Frank Slide, Alberta: The Day the Mountain Fell." www.sympatico.com.

57. *Tragedies of the Crowsnest Pass,* p. 36.

Chapter Five: Escape from Mount St. Helens

58. Quoted in *Volcano: The Eruption of Mount St. Helens.* Longview, WA: Longview Publishing, 1980, p. 15.
59. Quoted in Thomas E. Saarinen and James L. Sell, *Warning and Response to the Mount St. Helens Eruption.* Albany: State University of New York, 1985, p. 72.
60. Alwyn Scarth, *Vulcan's Fury.* New Haven, CT: Yale University Press, 1999, p. 2.
61. "The Day the Mountain Moved." www.thesunlink.com.
62. Quoted in Saarinen and Sell, *Warning and Response to the Mount St. Helens Eruption,* p. 85.
63. Quoted in Scarth, *Vulcan's Fury,* p. 219.
64. Quoted in "Buzz Smith Rises from the Ashes of a Volcano," *People Weekly,* March 15, 1999, p. 230.
65. Quoted in *Volcano: The Eruption of Mount St. Helens,* p. 77.
66. Quoted in *Volcano: The Eruption of Mount St. Helens,* p. 61.
67. Quoted in Mike Barber, "In Seconds, a Mountain and Many Lives Were Lost," *Seattle Post-Intelligencer,* May 8, 2000, no page given.
68. Quoted in "Buzz Smith Rises from the Ashes of a Volcano," p. 230.
69. Quoted in Scarth, *Vulcan's Fury,* p. 220.
70. Quoted in *Volcano: The Eruption of Mount St. Helens,* p. 59.
71. Quoted in Barber, "In Seconds, a Mountain and Many Lives Were Lost," no page given.
72. Quoted in Ralph Langer, ed., *Mount St. Helens Erupts.* Everett, WA: Daily Herald, 1980, p. 15.
73. Trixie Anders, "A Pilgrimage for Jim." http://geoweb.tamu.edu.

For Further Reading

Karen Magnuson Beil, *Fire in Their Eyes.* San Diego: Harcourt Brace, 1999. A book about wildfires and how they are fought.

Carmen Bredeson, *Mount St. Helens Volcano: Violent Eruption.* Berkeley Heights, NJ: Enslow, 2001.

Christopher Engholm, *The Armenian Earthquake.* San Diego: Lucent Books, 1989. A thorough description of the earthquake—its devastation, its origins, and its effects.

Allison Lassieur, *Earthquakes.* San Diego: Lucent Books, 2002. A thorough look at causes and effects of earthquakes, including stories of the most famous quakes in history.

Megan Stine, *They Survived Mount St. Helens.* New York: Random House, 1994. Describes the eruption of Mount St. Helens and the reactions of those who survived the disaster.

Paul Robert Walker, *Head for the Hills!* New York: Random House, 1993. A well-written and informative summary of the Johnstown Flood.

Anne Ylvisaker, *Landslides.* Mankato, MN: Capstone Books, 2003. Information on the causes and effects of landslides.

Works Consulted

Books

R.J. Blong, *Volcanic Hazards*. Sydney, Australia: Academic Press, 1984. A scholarly study of volcanoes and their effects. Useful for background; includes some information on Mount St. Helens.

Peter Briggs, *Rampage*. New York: David McKay, 1973. Useful background on floods that have struck the United States. Includes some information on the Johnstown tragedy of 1889.

Walter R. Brown and Billye W. McCutcheon, *Historical Catastrophes: Floods*. Reading, MA: Addison-Wesley, 1973. Includes a short chapter on Johnstown.

Hal Butler, *Nature at War*. Chicago: Henry Regnery, 1976. Descriptions of thirteen natural disasters in American history. Includes information on the Johnstown Flood.

Jelle Zeilinga de Boer and Donald Theodore Sanders, *Volcanoes in Human History*. Princeton, NJ: Princeton University Press, 2002. Descriptions of the impact of volcanoes, including Mount St. Helens.

Victor Heiser, *An American Doctor's Odyssey*. New York: W.W. Norton, 1936. Heiser was a survivor of the Johnstown Flood. His description of the flood takes up the first chapter of this autobiography.

Sebastian Junger, *Fire*. New York: W.W. Norton, 2001. A collection of essays by the author of *The Perfect Storm*. Includes one on the Storm King fire and another, earlier one on smoke-jumping. Both are useful.

J. William Kerr, *Frank Slide*. Calgary, Alberta, Canada: Barker, 1990. A short description of the 1903 Turtle Mountain landslide.

Ralph Langer, ed., *Mount St. Helens Erupts*. Everett, WA: Daily Herald, 1980. A book put together by staff members of a newspaper in Everett,

Washington. Includes good photos and insider accounts of the blast and its aftermath.

John N. Maclean, *Fire on the Mountain.* New York: William Morrow, 1999. A thorough and well-written account of the Storm King wildfire, including quotes and recollections from those firefighters who escaped.

Norman Maclean, *Young Men and Fire.* Chicago: University of Chicago Press, 1992. About the 1949 Mann Gulch fire in Montana. Useful for information about that fire and background on firefighting in general.

David G. McCullough, *The Johnstown Flood.* New York: Simon & Schuster, 1968. The best available account of the Johnstown Flood. Includes many direct quotes from survivors.

Leonard Palmer, *Mount St. Helens: The Volcano Explodes!* Portland, OR: Northwest Illustrated, 1980. Profusely illustrated and informative, if somewhat breathless in its writing. Palmer was a geologist working on Mount St. Helens data when the eruption occurred.

Yuri Rost, *Armenian Tragedy.* Trans. Elizabeth Roberts. New York: St. Martin's Press, 1990. A description of the 1988 Armenian earthquake, this book deals also with political and social unrest in and around Armenia during the time. Rost was a Soviet photojournalist who visited Armenia just after the earthquake struck.

Thomas E. Saarinen and James L. Sell, *Warning and Response to the Mount St. Helens Eruption.* Albany: State University of New York, 1985. An investigation of emergency procedures and planning during the Mount St. Helens explosion.

Alwyn Scarth, *Vulcan's Fury.* New Haven, CT: Yale University Press, 1999. A well-written and clear description of several powerful volcanic explosions, including Mount St. Helens. Informative, with good background material.

Murry A. Taylor, *Jumping Fire.* New York: Harcourt, 2000. Taylor fought fires as a smokejumper for many years. This is his description of his life in smokejumping.

Tragedies of the Crowsnest Pass. Surrey, British Columbia, Canada: Heritage House, 1983. Includes a description of the Frank Slide along with some background information on Frank and the region around it.

Volcano: The Eruption of Mount St. Helens. Longview, WA: Longview Publishing, 1980. The best of the journalistic-style books written about Mount St. Helens immediately after the disaster. Thorough and well illustrated, the book was put together by staff members of two Washington newspapers, one based only a few dozen miles from the volcano.

Wild Weather. Danbury, CT: Grolier, 1998. Contemporary articles and reports about natural disasters around the world. Includes useful information on the Frank Slide and the Johnstown Flood.

The World Almanac and Book of Facts 2003. New York: World Almanac Books, 2003. Useful for statistics on historical events.

Periodicals
Mike Barber, "In Seconds, a Mountain and Many Lives Were Lost," *Seattle Post-Intelligencer,* May 8, 2000.

"Buzz Smith Rises from the Ashes of a Volcano," *People Weekly,* March 15, 1999.

Fred Coleman, "A Land of the Dead," *Newsweek,* December 26, 1988.

Robert Davis et al., "Back into the 'Black,'" *USA Today,* July 8, 1994.

Darcy DeLeon, "Johnstown Recalls Terror of 1889 Flood," *USA Today,* May 31, 1989.

Bill Donahue et al., "Tragedy at Storm King," *American Forests,* January 1995.

Donald Dale Jackson, "When 20 Million Tons of Water Flooded Johnstown," *Smithsonian,* May 1989.

"The Killer Quake That Shook the World," *U.S. News & World Report,* December 19, 1988.

David Ludlum, "Our Most Infamous Natural Disaster," *Weatherwise,* April 1989.

Neil Modie, "Memories of Awesome Power, Silent Fury," *Seattle Post-Intelligencer*, May 15, 2000.

Laura Parker and William Prochnau, "Return to St. Helens," *USA Today,* May 17, 2000.

"The Day the Dam Broke," *Reader's Digest,* May 1989.

Allen Seager, "Frank Slide," *Beaver,* April/May 1996.

"Sorrow Felt Around World," *USA Today,* December 13, 1988.

"To Be Young Once, and Brave," *Time,* July 18, 1994.

"Vision of Horror," *Time,* December 26, 1988.

"When the Earth Shook," *Time,* December 19, 1988.

Internet Sources
Trixie Anders, "A Pilgrimage for Jim." http://geoweb.tamu.edu.

The 1988 "Armenian Earthquake."

www.clarkhumanities.org.

"Frank Slide, Alberta: The Day the Mountain Fell." A history of the Frank Slide. www.sympatico.ca.

Edwin Hutcheson, "A Brief History of the 1889 Johnstown Flood." www.jaha.org.

Personal accounts of the Mount St. Helens eruption. www.mtsthelens. net.

Personal accounts of the Mount St. Helens eruption. www.thesunlink. com.

Websites

Mount St. Helens National Volcanic Monument (www.fs.fed.us). General information and photos regarding the Mount St. Helens explosion.

National Landslide Information Center (http://landslides.usgs.gov). Sponsored by the United States Geological Survey, this site has useful links and information about landslides.

Only You Can Prevent Wildfires (www.smokeybear.com). Informative set of pages regarding wildfires, the science behind them, and methods of controlling them when they occur.

Index

Picture Credits

About the Author

Stephen Currie is the creator of Lucent's Great Escapes series. He has also written many other books for children and young adults, among them *Life in a Wild West Show* and *The Mississippi River,* both for Lucent. He lives in New York State with his wife and children. He enjoys kayaking, snowshoeing, and bicycling, but has never yet had to escape from a natural disaster.